THE ADVENTURES OF CARTER AND THE LAST DRAGON

by

JOHN E. PARNELL

TABLE OF CONTENTS

CHAPTER ONE

Carter Receives His Grandpa's Gifts and is Transported to a New Land, Where He Meets a Dragon Named Azi.

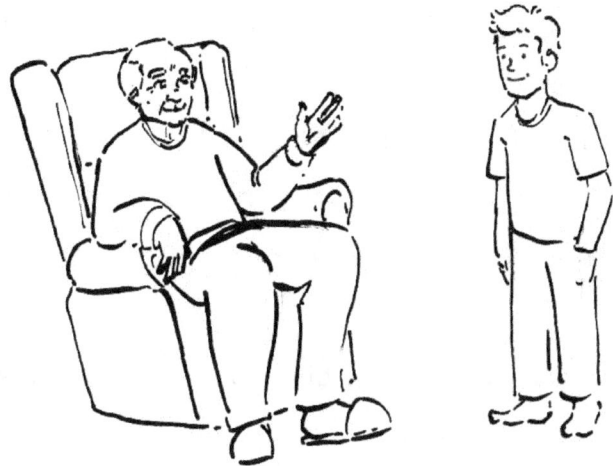

I keep wondering when my parents would understand that I'm not possessed by some kind of strange spirit all because of my love for magic. I enjoy going about the house muttering words I don't even understand. Well, everyone thinks that I'm weird, except for my Grandpa, of course. It's like he's the only person who understands the power behind imagination.

My Grandpa is my favorite. Even though he's old, he still has a lot of imagination in him. Both of my parents already ran out of theirs. They forgot the importance of it all. Whenever they see me running around the house to escape from the evil magician or a sinking ship, they think I'm crazy. Dad always yells at me at the top of his lungs, telling me to stop running around the house before I break something. He's not even worried about my getting injured!

He doesn't understand that the expensive vase on the counter isn't really there, so I can't possibly break it. I know that he doesn't realize that in fact, it isn't an expensive vase, but a red crystal. A very powerful one. He doesn't understand any of that. He doesn't understand that if I don't break the red crystal, the evil magician's powers will never leave, and I'll be trapped in the world of lava forever. Sometimes, I feel like my dad just doesn't care about my safety. Not at all.

My mom is more understanding than my dad is. She tells me that as long as I'm careful, she doesn't care how close I get to the red crystal. I think she believes me. Or even if she doesn't, she doesn't think that I'm crazy. I don't know how, but I think she knows that the red crystal can't be broken into pieces. The only way it stops giving power to the magician is if it's turned upside down. That way, the energy can't come out of the top of it.

Normally, the magician's two-headed servant would always stop me! He barks at me until he has my attention, then he uses his powers of mind control to make me come to him. He'll take me to a secluded place and punish me for my interfering with order. Most times, I try to resist, but he ends up overcoming me. Other times, I would wrestle so hard, as if I'd get a trophy for winning. But when my Grandpa sees me playing my games, he asks me to hurry up and finish, so that I can tell him about my adventures. He loves to hear about all the inventive scenarios I can dream up in my free time.

There was one I told him about, that he really liked. In the adventure, I used my artistic skills to draw a three-headed dragon on the ground, using a nail. The piece was really beautiful. All of a sudden, it sprang up and started chasing me. The chase was swift and when I got tired, I stopped abruptly, daring to face the dragon. He was probably overwhelmed by my boldness, and he didn't attack me. We became friends instantly like we've known each other for ages. I smiled happily as it faded away slowly, eventually vanishing into thin air. I decided to name it Tray. I still see it in my imagination.

Another interesting one was about this large eagle that was attacked by a snake. After several hours of trying to break free, an eagle got hold of the snake and flew up high into the sky, changing the battlefield. The eagle released the snake and it went crashing into the ground. I was so excited. I had never seen such a thing before.

These things appealed so much to my senses. I absolutely loved it. This was something new, something different. These adventures filled me with happiness and enthusiasm. I wanted to see more, I wanted to discover more of the amazing land of dreams and imagination.

Oh, and how about the shark and the whale? They were fighting over a common territory: the sea. Both wanted to claim it as his own, but there had to be something to determine the victor. The test was that the two animals would stay away from water for a few days. In a twinkle of an eye, the days passed and neither of them survived it. Their folks wailed as I smiled back to life.

Whenever we go to visit Grandpa, there isn't much for me to do, since my parents spend so much time making sure he's okay. That's why I have to find ways to entertain myself. And then, when I am too tired to imagine any more things, he would tell me a story of his own. But Grandpa's stories are very different from mine. Grandpa says they are real.

A long time ago, dragons and humans used to live together in peace. They played, grew up, worked, and died together. In many instances, dragons and humans that were born at the same time were paired together for life. The pairs were revered by the ancient people. But for the structure of the two creatures, one wouldn't even know the difference between them with the kind of bond they shared. The dragons were very fond of the humans and would go any length to protect their friends from harm. They would even kill, just to keep the humans safe.

There were moments when they would all assemble, especially when the moon was out, to discuss issues relating to their well-being and the likes. The dragons taught them simple tricks they could apply to defeat their enemies. Like, when battling with a snake, its head should be the major aim to strike at. Once the head was successfully severed, the rest of the body would become easier to deal with.

By cutting off the head, the snake would not be able to bite, thereby preventing harm to the humans or dragons. The humans were also taught that the snake's venom was very poisonous and dangerous and it could cause death. Once the venom reaches the heart, that's the end of the victim.

So, the trick is that a piece of cloth should be tied tightly around the area where the person was bitten, in order to stop the flow of blood at that spot, then, the venom needs to be pressed out. Special herbs used to treat snake bites would be administered, by squeezing the liquid out and applying it on the wound. The humans were always happy to receive lectures like these, because they were very prone to attacks and were always dependent on the dragons for their safety.

The dragons also taught the humans to beware of scorpions. The baby scorpions were the deadliest and they always looked forward to stinging their victims. The scorpions possessed two large front pincers and a curved tail with a poisonous stinger in the end. Those parts of the scorpion should be attacked simultaneously.

Whenever there was a victim of scorpion bite, the preventive measures to avoid death were similar to those of the snake, because the scorpion's sting was equally poisonous. A cloth would be tied tightly around the spot to prevent the venom from flowing to the heart. In addition, in the case of a scorpion sting another important advice was that the victim should be immediately made to chew onions. The onions should also be used to clean the surface of the wound. Then the victim would be fine. These things appeared to be magic to the humans. They were surprised that little things like that could save a life.

But technology started to grow, and people became less dependent on the dragons. The dragons started to feel betrayed. They felt more so, especially because they couldn't even attribute to this new development, and it wasn't even their fault. It was like all of a sudden these changes happened, and they didn't understand what happened. They had done nothing wrong to warrant this hostility

. The new technological development had eaten deep into their senses. The humans started making it obvious that the dragons were not, and could never be like them, no matter how hard they tried. The humans started to see them as a means to an end and developed machines that could harness the dragons' power.

You see, the dragons were a peaceful race and would never rebel against the humans. They were very loyal creatures. Many of them died during experiments or because too much of their energy was drained from them. Soon enough, the dragons had had enough. They couldn't bear it anymore. They ran away, forever hiding from humans.

"That's amazing, Grandpa!"

Oh, well, it gets even better. Grandpa actually knows one of those dragons. He saved one back then, when he was just a young boy like me. His father had sent him to gather some firewood. Being a vibrant young boy, he happily ran off to get the job done. A short distance away from the area where he intended to gather the wood from, he was able to see two figures wrestling.

He hid behind a tree and he saw that it was a dragon and a human. It was obvious that the dragon was being chased from a very long distance and was panting heavily. It was even begging for mercy. Grandpa had always been an impartial person ever since his boyhood. He moved a bit closer and he was able to hear the words both parties were uttering. He figured out that the human was a hunter, who was fortunate enough to capture the dragon and they had been in the forest for days.

The hunter promised to release the dragon only with some conditions. He used some supernatural powers to hypnotize the dragon, which then enabled him to direct and control the creature. He made the dragon hunt for several kinds of animals, as per his command. He also made the dragon cut down various pieces of wood, which he intended to take home.

He was using the dragon to do work for him, and the human even rode on the dragon, as if it was a horse. He also forcefully made the dragon teach him skills that were strictly secluded to the dragon world and now forbidden for humans. The human made things really difficult for his victim, not giving him a chance to defend himself.

After all that, the hunter refused to let the dragon go because he was mean and selfish. He found something that has been lost for a long time, and thought that the dragon would be his personal gold mine. It would do anything he wanted, for as long as he wanted. He wanted to take the dragon home, just to show him off and boost his ego. He hoped to be named as one of the best hunters in the land. He didn`t have many good qualities to say the least, so he thought that this was his only chance at becoming famous and rich.

Thereafter, the dragon tried to gather up the last bits of power left in him and made an attempt to escape, which led to the chase. When the dragon got tired of running, he stopped and turned to wrestle with the hunter. It was that point when Grandpa spotted them. Being a very brilliant boy, he could understand what was happening.

From his childhood, he had a sense of justice. He hated anything pertaining to injustice and he would do anything to counter injustice. That was exactly what he did. He had so much pity for the poor dragon who was lamenting vigorously about his predicament.

Grandpa cleverly maneuvered his way to the spot without being noticed, and with his cutlass, he stabbed the hunter from behind. He was a boy filled with energy and strength even beyond his age. My Grandpa quickly took the dragon by his hand and fled the scene, while the wicked hunter groaned in pain. When they were almost out of sight, he heard footsteps moving towards the hunter. He was glad that the hunter might be saved from dying. As much as he loved justice, he wouldn't want to cause another's death. That's Grandpa for you!

As they were fleeing, the dragon became really exhausted and couldn't run anymore. Grandpa carried him and looked for a shed where he could take the dragon to. He had learned that dragons ate plants and bugs. He quickly got some and fed the dragon with them. He also got water from a nearby stream. He got herbs from the bush, which he squeezed to treat the dragon's wounds.

He knew he was taking too long already and he would be in trouble with his parents, his mum especially, but he damned the consequences of his late return just for the dragon. He had this fiery boldness once he was set to save a soul. He allowed the dragon to sleep as he watched over him like a guardian angel. From his act, one would not even know that dragons and humans were enemies. It brought back memories of old times, when things were different.

When the dragon finally woke up, he was feeling well already and according to their nature, once they get refreshed, they get all their powers back. It was something supernatural. That dragon was so grateful that humans still had goodness left in them, and he told Grandpa how to find him if he ever needed the dragon's help. The dragon hoped to return the favor once, thanking Grandpa for saving his life.

Grandpa`s stories about the age of dragons are always the best. He told me once about a time when there were lots of dragons around, but as time passed they became fewer when people became hostile to them. Some died of old age, while others had to hide from danger.

None of them were left, except for a little one who was no bigger than a little boy; a little boy like Joey, who lived in a town where the weather changed with the seasons. Every fall, his family would pack all their belongings and move to a region where it would be warm in the winter.

Joey hated the moving thing so much. He found it really uncomfortable. So, the next time his parents wanted to move, he resisted vehemently and told them he preferred to stay at home. His mother tried so hard to convince him, telling him that they would risk freezing to death if they didn't move, but Joey wouldn't listen, because he had never witnessed it. Joey told his parents that it was just a myth like dragons and unicorns, because, on several occasions he had heard people say it. His parents nevertheless told him that winter was real, as well as were unicorns and dragons.

Joey stubbornly refused to go with them and he went to hide, so that his absence would not be noticed. Joey however regretted staying back as the cold dealt with him seriously. He went through hell and he almost froze to death. Just in the nick of time, he heard the door open.

He rushed there, hoping his parents had come back for him, but to his surprise, he found a little dragon staring at him. Joey angrily questioned the dragon on who he was and what he was doing there.

The dragon replied that he was called Presh and that he was the only dragon left there. He said that he always stayed there when humans went to a warm region for the winter. Joey had no choice, but to confess his condition and miserable state to the dragon. The dragon then pitied him. He decided that he would save the boy. Presh had to breathe some warm air on to Joey to help him get warm.

Joey was overwhelmed by Presh's kind gesture and they quickly became friends. They kept each other company and Presh did not cease to keep Joey warm. When winter was about to be over, Joey didn't want Presh to leave, but at the same time, he wouldn't have been able to give a reasonable explanation about being friends with a dragon, whom people did not even believe existed.

Later, they decided to build a house for Presh in the basement, so he could be safe. On their return, Joey's parents were surprised to see him alive, as they thought he would have frozen to death. They were overwhelmed by joy and relief, and wanted to know all the details about Joey's miraculous survival.

Joey explained all that transpired and they wanted to meet Presh. They met him and asked him to stay with them. And he did. The next winter, Joey's family stayed at home while Presh kept them warm. Word soon spread that there was a dragon in town, and people wanted to see this miracle for themselves, as they didn't believe it.

Everyone was surprised, and the town-people realized eventually that this could be a good thing. Subsequently, the whole town wanted to have a dragon of their own and Presh made the dragons come back. Shortly afterwards, the dragons multiplied and were welcomed into everyone's home. Still, some people insisted that dragons were a myth. But Joey and Presh knew best.

I loved the story so much I was wishing I was Joey in the story. I don't know why, but there's this link I have with dragons. I love them so much. I always liked hearing stories about them, their nature, how they grow, their features, how they feed, and their powers. This interested me the most. Grandpa taught me that dragons could spit fire from their mouths. That's simply amazing. He also told me that they are very fast and swift in nature and they are very strong. They are like other exotic animals: sometimes useful and protective; other times harmful and dangerous (when they are made to exhibit that part of them).

Grandpa also told me that another development that strained the relationship between humans and dragons was Christianity.

When Christianity spread across the world, dragons took on a decidedly sinister interpretation and came to represent Satan. Dragons were described as possessing unusual strength, an outer coat which is very difficult to strip off, an impenetrable double coat or armor, a mouth so well shielded with doors and ringed about with fearsome teeth, a back that had rows of shields tightly sealed together; with each so close to the next that no air can pass between, they are joined fast to one another, they cling together and cannot be parted.

A dragon's snorting throws out flashes of light; its eyes are like rays of dawn. Flames streamed from its mouth; sparks of fire shoot out. Smoke poured from its nostrils as from a boiling pot over boiling reeds. Its breath set coals ablaze and flames darted from its mouth. But I wasn't scared of them, no. In fact, I always thought that Grandpa's tales about the age of dragons were just awesome. He also told me that the belief in dragons was based not just in legend but also in hard evidence. The people of the old days were filled with so many traditions that are lost today.

My grandfather is lost today, too.

"Poor, old, crazy, and lovable, still believing in dragons," people would say when Grandpa was still alive.

I even heard some people gossip that he was probably mentally retarded, while some people said he was possessed by some kind of unknown spirit. Some others said it was a sign of old age and that old people were prone to all kinds of stupid beliefs, and that he was close to his grave. I was very angry when hearing those kinds of stupid remarks about my own Grandpa, whom I revered and cherished so much. My Grandpa, whom I held in high esteem and looked up to. He was the only one who was always ready to listen to my dragonish imaginations. I vowed to retaliate, but Grandpa stopped me. He said that was typical of people who lacked the understanding of a subject matter and who were ignorant of certain facts.

Now that he's dead, they no longer make fun of his beliefs. I don't know what I'll do without him. Grandpa was the one person who could brighten up any day, and now he's gone. Who do I have to share my fantasies with? Who will hear the adventures of the wizards now, or give me tips on how to avoid the lava ground?

"You have to grow up eventually, Carter. I know you love your stories, but they are just stories," my mother smiled at me when she said this.

Mum doesn't understand that for me, my imaginations and adventures about dragons are beyond stories. There is this bond and connection in the darkest parts of my heart and soul. I just feel that they shouldn't have been treated the way they were, and shouldn't have been forgotten. My Grandpa shouldn't be forgotten, either.

If growing up means that I need to forget our adventures together, our stories, then I never want to grow up. Tears streamed down my face as I started reminiscing about the times I shared with Grandpa. I remembered those times we discussed issues relating to dragons. He told me his level of affiliation with these creatures.

There were times we did experiments together, as if we were magicians. Good old days.

"Besides, Grandpa isn't gone just yet," dad said.

I tried so much to figure out what my dad meant by that statement. Did he mean to say that Grandpa did not die? No, we all attended the burial and I saw my dear Grandpa in the coffin during the lying-in state, when people were asked to go around the coffin and pay their last respect. So, how's it possible that he did *not* die?

Oh, I've heard several stories of people dying and coming back to life, but all these were myths and only Jesus could do that. He did that when he was on Earth. And as it was only possible for him, I discarded that thought as well. Grandpa couldn't have been resurrected from the dead.

"He left you something," Dad's voice rang into my ears and I was awakened from my thoughts.

"What do you mean?" I asked my dad, while wiping a tear from my eye.

He simply replied with a smile, which suggested good news. I'm so used to my dad that I understand what every expression he makes means. That smile wasn't strange to me. I just hoped it was something that would make my worries about Grandpa vanish. I didn't know Grandpa had a present for me. I waited while my parents headed upstairs where the gift was. I thought and thought, as far as my mind could stretch, but I couldn't imagine what it could be. Fortunately, I didn't have to wait long.

My parents came downstairs, carrying a small wooden box. I

quickly opened it to find a pocketknife, a ring and an old key inside. I'd seen the pocketknife more than enough times, so I knew it well. Grandpa always had it with him, and it always seemed to come handy.

I had asked him on several occasions to tell me what it was meant for, but he wouldn't tell me. He would reassure me that it was just a matter of time for me to know what it was used for. The ring was a little more mysterious to me, although it was beautiful. Even though Grandpa always wore it, he never let anyone else touch it. In fact, he rarely touched it himself, which seemed a bit strange to me. And even when he did, he was very careful about it, as if it was more than just a simple ring. At that time, I already figured out that there was more to it and it was anything but ordinary. However, its true nature was beyond my imagination.

Most mysterious to me was the key. He only ever showed it to me once, but no one else had ever seen it. These were his most prized possessions. I glowed with happiness as I felt honored. He entrusted these possessions in my care.

"Thank you," I whispered to my parents.

These things meant more to Grandpa than anything else. It was now my responsibility to take care of them. The pocketknife and ring were easy. All I had to do was keep the knife in my pocket and the ring on my finger.

I glanced at the ring one more time before I put it on, then I screamed out, "Ring of the dragons, activate!"

Although I had no idea whether this would work or not, it seemed like the most appropriate name for it. Grandpa's dragon stories were always the best, and I needed something to refer to it as such. I wanted to make sure that looking at that ring would ensure that I never forget our adventures together. Little did I know that wearing the ring wasn`t just going to connect me to my memories of the dragons and grandpa, but it was also like a gateway into my own imagination.

I had always wished to have mysterious objects that could further enhance my imagination. The last I had was a small pair of glasses. Grandpa gave them to me many years ago, because I wouldn't let him rest, constantly asking for the object. I thought that I just got the best gift in the world. I would wear the glasses and begin to see all sorts of things.

There were times I saw some flying dragons fighting in the air. The sight was hilarious and I couldn't help but laugh. Before I knew it, other dragons had gathered to cheer on the parties. It reminded me of my primary school days, where two people were fighting and before you could spell JACKIE ROBINSON, a large crowd would gather to cheer on the parties, like it was something to be happy about.

The supporters would divide themselves and chant the names of the parties. Some would just support the winning party. No one would intervene until someone of authority, like a teacher, appeared. In a flash, everyone would disappear and the fighting parties would be left to face the consequences of their actions. And this is exactly what happened amongst the dragons, except for one tony difference: this time the opponents weren't humans, but dragons.

But again, if this happened at the time when dragons and humans were equal, just like Grandpa said, there would be no difference really. It seemed like my fighting dragons would not stop. Each wanted to show that he was stronger than the other. And I found this behavior to be very humanlike.

Suddenly, a messenger of the king of dragons appeared. One could tell he was a king's messenger from the clothes he had on and the staff he was holding. His appearance alone commanded respect, as he was representing the king. In a flash, they had disappeared and everything was clear and plain as ever. I couldn't stop laughing.

"What's so funny?" my mum's voice went straight into my ears and I jerked back to reality.

It was then that I realized I had been dreaming all along. It all seemed so real, and most of the times I didn't know that they were only fantasies. Mum was used to it tough. There are times I would just utter words she didn't understand from my sleep.

I pushed those thoughts aside and once again concentrated on my lovely ring. Suddenly, I could see so many marvelous things. Transparent flashes of dragons flew across the room and beautiful river streamed through the house. It was like I was staring directly into someone else's fantasy world. It was amazing. Could it have been Grandpa's secret fantasy land?

"I guess some things never change," my dad laughed.

"Don't forget the key, son."

"I won't," I said, lifting the key from the box and returning the empty box to my parents.

"I have to find the secret door it unlocks. I can't open the door if I lose the key."

The sadness from my Grandpa's death was now slowly drifting away. The artifacts he had left me gave me peace. It's almost like I could feel his hand on my shoulder, reassuring me that everything would be OK. It was nearly as if I suddenly understood what my father meant earlier. I felt connected to Grandpa, as if he was still in the room with me. He let me share his imagination, and for that I was very grateful.

"Go, Ring of Dragons!" I said as I stroked the simple ring with two of my fingers.

To my surprise, a light shot out from it, streaming up the stairs. I chased after the light as fast as possible, avoiding all manners of exotic plants and animals. I was careful not to lose sight of the light as it traveled in several circles upstairs, before shooting under the door that was leading into Grandpa's room. I crawled beneath a stone to follow the light into a dark camber.

The light disappeared behind the door to Grandpa's closet. This wasn't making sense anymore, but I couldn't back off. Not at this point. Without thinking, I pulled the key from my pocket and inserted it into the lock. I didn't know what to expect, but the sense of adventure there was incredible. I couldn't walk away from it. When I turned the key in the lock, the door swung open all by itself and sucked me into a pool of light.

Fear gripped me at first, but Grandpa had taught me that one of the greatest qualities that any real man should possess is boldness. Remembering this, I shook off my fears and walked boldly in, daring to face whatever was coming my way. I was still walking, not know-ing exactly where I was going. When my strength couldn't take it anymore, I decided to rest. I sat under a baobab tree, as I enjoyed the cool breeze. I felt calm and relaxed, and my previous tension and fear completely disappeared.

Suddenly, I heard something hiss very close to my head. I ig-nored it, but then I heard it again and again. It was then that I turned to find a very large cobra staring at me. I couldn't afford to be afraid this time. This was war! I quickly scanned around with my eyes to look for something to fight with. I found a brownish object that had the shape of a tooth, with a very sharp and pointed edge. I took it and pointed it at the snake.

But I couldn't just rush into it, no. Grandpa had taught me that for every war, there would be a strategy and it is significant to strategize before one can win a battle. I decided to stab the snake's eyes first so that I would be able to defeat it, and it wouldn't see me anymore. I did exactly that, and it seemed to be working. I was win-ning! Feeling proud of myself, I got a very large stick from a branch of the tree with which I hit the snake. After rigorous beating and tor-turing, I finally killed the snake. Satisfied, I pushed it far away and continued resting. I still had my weapon in my hands and I studied it closely, trying to figure out what it was.

As if by some miracle, Grandpa appeared next to me, and he smiled down at me as he asked, "Do you know what that is?"

I shook my head. I was happy Grandpa was there with me. He told me that it was a dragon's tooth. An expression of confusion and surprise was evident on my face, but Grandpa knew exactly what I was going through.

I asked how it was possible to get the tooth of a dragon. Grandpa explained that dragons weren't just useful during their lifetime. They were very useful even after their death. Their body parts could be fashioned into various materials.

This was one of the reasons I loved Grandpa, he always had something new and interesting to tell me. He said that the dragon's set of teeth were very sharp and could be used to cut anything. He also told me that the dragon's heartstring was exceptionally powerful, and one of the most common kinds of core used in wands.

I also learned from Grandpa that dragon hide could be used to make clothing. The skin was very tough, impervious to some spells, and provided the same physical protection as leather, while at the same time having the same texture and appearance as snake skin. Dragon hide was used to make gloves, boots, jackets and shields. He also said that dragon eggs were used by witches and wizards to make spells, but they were very difficult to get.

"Grandpa, this is amazing!" I squealed happily.

Grandpa told me to scan around for as many dragon parts I could find. It was then I realized truly that I was in a dragon land.

"Who the hell are you?" a voice rang harshly into my ears.

My eyes opened immediately and I realized it had been a dream all along. No wonder, I had been thinking of Grandpa so much that I couldn't help but see him in my dreams. I looked up to see who cut short my chat with Grandpa. And right before me was a dragon, a young dragon. Before I could even mutter anything, the stern look of his face warned me to be careful of whatever I had to say. I decided to keep the ring, my Grandpa and everything else a secret for now. Until I knew what I was up against.

So, I simply replied, "I'm Carter."

He didn't even spare me the next question.

"What do you want?" he asked like he was the owner of the land.

At that point, I realized that I did not actually know what I wanted. It was evident that he was tired of the whole drama, as he slapped my face. It was then that I realized the true meaning of trespassing. This was the dragon land I had been dreaming about and here was a young dragon staring into my face.

The dragon spoke very harshly to me, accusing me of being a spy for wicked humans like myself. He dragged me onto the ground and threatened to kill me, if I did not tell him about the true nature of my mission. I was too dumbfounded to say anything. I just surrendered, as he continued to drag me back and forth.

Grandpa had taught me that another war strategy is to pretend like you don't know how to fight at first, and take time to study your opponent to know where to strike. That was exactly what I was doing until he pushed my hands up, ready to throw me away. He just stopped abruptly and I noticed the change in his look. It was a mixture of surprise and questioning. One could tell he had a lot of questions that begged for answers.

"Where did you get that?" he yelled.

I replied, "What?"

He pointed to the shining object around my finger. He was referring to Grandpa's ring.

I told him it was a gift from my Grandpa. At this point, he became a bit interested in my mission. I told him how I got to the dragon land and how the gifts helped me. I told him about Grandpa and his love for dragons. The dragon must have decided to believe me, as he told me to call him Azi.

Azi told me how much every dragon hated humans due to the torture they were subjected to. He told me the only human they could relate to was the owner of that ring, which was Grandpa.

"He was the only human who was good to us, until the moment he disappeared," Azi confessed sadly.

He told me of how Grandpa was Azi`s father, Dara's dear friend. Grandpa was the only human Azi and Dara trusted, according to Azi. He said that all other humans were either afraid of dragons and attacked them on sight, or tried to capture them for their powers. Dragons had been hunted until only he and Dara were left.

I was curious to hear more and I asked him where Dara was. I could see the bitter look on his face as he told me that, a few weeks before, a dragon hunter had found Dara and tried to capture him. He told me that Dara escaped, but he was severely injured. The wounds he sustained deteriorated and eventually killed him. I could feel his pain even as he talked. Ever since then, he had been alone in the land. Azi further told me that the most annoying part was that the crazy hunter wouldn't back off. He was still hell-bent on looking for Azi. I told him the place wasn't safe for him anymore and he agreed. He told me he wanted to try to find the land in the south that legends say was a sanctuary for dragons, but he needed serious help to do that.

"I hoped to ask our friend for help since he knew as much dragon lore as Dara had," Azi said soberly.

A wave of pity swept through me and I was determined in my heart to help him out. This whole drama started making sense to me. That was why Grandpa gave me the three gifts. He believed in me so much and my love for dragons. He thought that I could save the last dragon escape certain death.

"I can help you." I said to Azi's utter surprise.

He asked, "How would you do that?"

I tried to convince him that since we were two individuals, we were a team, and we would work things out. But I knew that there was more to it than just being a team. I had no idea what our next step should be, all I knew is that I wanted to help Azi. At that point, I wished Grandpa was actually there to apply his own wealth of knowledge and help me fulfil my true destiny…

CHAPTER TWO

Carter and Azi Are Chased by A Dragon Hunter.

Azi and I were still trying to reason things out together when we suddenly heard noises nearby. The ever inquisitive me was still trying to trace what the noise was and where it was coming from. Little did I know that we were in imminent danger.

Azi pulled me and did not have to tell me to come before I took to my heels. We ran to a different spot entirely. He warned me that the noises we heard earlier suggested that the dragon hunter was getting closer and that was dangerous. I couldn't really figure out why Azi could not let us stay and fight with this dragon hunter once and for all. It was as if he knew what was running through my mind when he began to tell me the extent of the dragon hunter's wickedness. He said the hunter is very desperate and had no mercy at all. He killed several dragons and sold some of them out.

"Korvis is evil!" Azi screamed in pain.

Azi also told me that he feared he might not be able to do a proper burial for Dara, as he had been on the run to escape from the hunter whom he called Korvis. His greatest fear was, however, the mutilation of Dara's body. In the sense that, if Korvis discovers the dead body of Dara, he would totally dismember the body parts and cart them away. That was the level of the hunter's ruthlessness. Just as we were speaking of the devil, Azi drew my attention to the beast some miles away and his greatest fear exactly was being manifested. As Korvis thrusted his cutlass into Dara's body, Azi couldn't help but weep, for it was like his own body.

Just the way I was very close to Grandpa, so was Azi to his father. Now, I remembered vividly my dream when I got to the land, where Grandpa was telling me about the usefulness of a dragon's body parts. This was the exact manifestation of his teachings. It was as if I was watching a horror movie. Korvis first scrapped Dara's skin; he even had a jar to collect some blood he took out of the skin. I remember Grandpa telling me that those skins are very tough and could be used for physical protection as leather, that they could be used to make gloves, boots, jackets and shields. Korvis would surely sell the blood to witches and wizards to make their spells. Quickly, he tore Dara's mouth open and he removed the dragon's teeth. I remembered that it was this weapon that saved me from the cobra earlier. What would I have done without it? Korvis further dissected his victim. He sliced out his heartstring, which Grandpa told me was very powerful to make magic wands. We watched as the evil hunter further examined Dara's body to see other parts he could cut out.

Obviously, he was enjoying it as he beat is chest vigorously like winners do. He started scrapping the decomposing elements and scales on the skin. When he had done that satisfactorily, he started slicing the remains of Dara's body into smaller bits.

Azi couldn't hold back his disgust as he watched this humiliation. It led him to scream out, loud enough for Korvis to hear. Azi was so angry and determined to attack Korvis, but I knew better that it was a dangerous thing to do. No! Never would I allow Azi to get hurt.

I pulled him away and we started running again. But it was too late, Korvis started chasing us.

I don't think I'd ever run like that all my life. As we fled, different thoughts were running through my mind. I thought about the possibility of Korvis catching up with us. That's death automatically and Azi's hope of getting to the South where other dragons are would be defeated. No! That would not happen. I intensified my efforts and I motivated Azi as well. As we ran, Azi was also whispering to me that we could make it. Korvis was far behind us but he could still see us. The way he panted heavily was enough to scare a person. This hunter was fierce, determined to catch up with his victims.

As we ran, I wasn't even thinking straight anymore, neither was I looking at where I was going, all I had to do was run! I ran into some entangled twigs and they clustered around my legs so tightly that it hindered my movement. I staggered and fell flat on the ground. Azi had gone on for a bit before he realized I wasn't with him and Korvis was just few miles behind me. Azi was stuck. If he came back to help me, we both would be in trouble. If he doesn't, then he'd be safe and I alone will suffer. Korvis was getting close now, and to my uttermost surprise, Azi ran back to me just as the hunter's cutlass was getting close to me.

"Get on my back!" Azi screamed.

Without wasting time, I obeyed quickly and off we went into the air.

I was surprised Azi could fly. I had heard of flying dragons but I did not think Azi could fly. I felt happy on his back as we flew into the air until we couldn't see Korvis anymore. We finally landed under a mahogany tree. It was more like a fall than a landing anyway because Azi was very exhausted.

"Thank you," was all I could say as tears streamed down my cheeks.

I did not believe he could take such pains just to save me. I thought a part of him still harbored that hatred he has for humans for me too. I felt loved. I can trust him with my life.

Azi smiled as he echoed, "You're welcome."

I asked why he did not tell me about his ability to fly. He told me he had been warned by Dara not to disclose it to any human except in special circumstances because they could not afford to trust any human, except Grandpa of course. He also said that taking flight was a risk, because he had been told that he had to grow to a certain stage before he could fly. But he could not just watch me die like that, so he took the risk.

Azi felt Korvis was in fact an animal that should never live with humans with the way he was cutting Dara earlier. Azi said it was a surprise to him that he survived after Dara's death. He thought he'd just die too because of the bond between them. Azi told me of how his mother died when he was still very little. She was captured by humans and her powers were extracted. She was killed shortly after that. He recalled how she loved him and was ready to do anything to protect him from harm. Her name was Tara. What a beautiful name!

He said his father had ever since been supportive and made sure he did not feel the impact of his mother's death. He taught Azi the powers of a dragon and how to use them. His father was in fact his confidant. Azi also told me about Grandpa, how he saved them from humans and how he would constantly check on their well-being. We wept together as I thought about my Grandpa.

How I wish he were still alive to help us. I would've loved to meet the great Dara but, unfortunately, the evil hunter had gotten rid of him. Azi asked about my parents and their view towards dragons. I laughed at first and told him that my parents didn't categorically disbelieve in their existence. They however know dragons exist.

I told him of how my dad would scream at the top of his lungs just so that I wouldn't break something; how my parents thought that I was possessed with some kind of spirit not knowing I'm merely driven by my imagination. They both had run out of theirs. How my Grandpa was my only confidant and the one who was always ready to share my inventive adventures with him, how Grandpa would go any lengths to tell me stories about dragons. I told him of how the magician's two-headed servant in the red crystal would stop me and bark at me until he has my attention, then used his powers of mind control to make me come to him. Thereafter, he would take me to a secluded place and punish me for my interference. I told him the best stories I heard from Grandpa. I told him the one about Joey, the little boy who refused to go with his family to a warm region during winter, and how his dragon friend, Presh, helped him to survive the brutal cold by giving him enough heat to keep warm.

Azi was glad I lovingly had things to say about dragons. He, however, told me that Dara had once told him that dragons were not altogether faultless. He told him of dragons who were made to be wicked, especially ones used for protection.

He said Dara had told him the story of a dragon who was a friend of a king, and he protected the palace. The king wanted to travel for a long period and his little princess would be alone in the palace. He therefore told the dragon to keep watch over his little princess. The dragon was very happy and he did the job diligently. He made sure no harm came to the princess. Over the years, the dragon grew so big that he was able to shield the whole palace. Nobody could gain access to the palace, not even the king himself. It became a tug of war, but the dragon was eventually defeated.

We chatted more and more, feeling more comfortable with each other. Azi's countenance suddenly changed, and I asked him what the problem was. He told me that he was really bothered about the whole adventure; how we would survive; how we would permanently escape from Korvis and get to our destination. Even though I did not know much about how we could achieve that, I told him not to worry and that we would be fine. We were already hungry so we gathered some bugs and plants for Azi to feed on since that's what dragons eat. We were also able to hunt a small animal which we roasted with Azi's fire. I ate that.

We decided to sleep and wake up early the next morning to continue with our adventure and that was what we did. The next morning, we continued our adventure.

We chatted happily as we moved on. Suddenly, we heard cries few yards away from where we were. We stopped at first and tried to figure out what was causing the cry, but we just couldn't figure it out. Just then, Azi laughed. I asked him what was funny and he told me he knew the creatures that were crying. He called them "Bush Babies." He told me they are funny creatures who are fond of crying in the jungle. He then told me to go with him so I could see what they looked like. As we moved closer, the bush babies took to their heels. We continued with our trip as Azi further told me more interesting facts about these things called bush babies. He told me that they have very distinctive forward facing eyes that are enormous and those eyes are so large in relation to their head that they cannot move them in their sockets. If they want to shift their gaze, they have to turn their whole head. Consequently, they are able to look directly backward over their shoulders. I was mesmerized by this quick revelation. It was surely adding to my wealth of knowledge.

I couldn't help but ask Azi, "How did they get the name BUSH BABY?"

Azi told me that despite its small size, it was a very vocal little animal. They give a range of calls ranging from grunts to chicks and crackles. Their long-range, territorial call sounds just like a wailing human child. Azi said a combination of that with the "cute" face may account for their name.

I wasn't ready to drop this subject as I found it really interesting, so I told Azi to tell me more. He then told me that using its large ears, a bush baby can locate a prey by a sound so precisely that it could catch flying insects in the air. He also said that they were fast, agile and very accurate, and that allowed them to catch insect prey in the dark by snatching them from the air. I was wondering how these creatures would mark their territories considering their feeble nature. Azi further explained to me that, in line with their nocturnal habits, bush babies made heavy use of scent signals. They have an unusual and elaborate way of scent marking, which is "urine washing." This process involves dribbling urine over their hands and feet and then rubbing them together. They leave a trail of damp, smelly foot and hand prints along their pathways as they move through the branches. This way, they are able to mark their territories.

Azi also told me that the way they breed is quite different from other creatures. The males check the reproductive condition of females by sniffing their genitals. Males fight savagely and a loser that cannot escape may be killed. A female in heat aggressively repulses the male's first approaches. When she does finally allow the male to approach, mating takes place repeatedly for about five minutes every two hours. A mother stays continuously with her babies for their first three days. The young are weaned at six weeks and are independent at two months. Young males disperse a few kilometers from their birthplace, while females often remain in their natal group.

"Wow!" was all I could say.

"How did you know all this?" I asked Azi and he smiled saying Dara taught him.

We decided to take a break and talk more about accomplishing our mission this time. We were approaching the human territory which meant danger for Azi. I couldn't watch Azi get hurt, so I told him we would move through fairly unoccupied countryside, where small villages are a decent distance from each other and easy to avoid.

"Whether Korvis or anyone liked it or not, we would overcome! We'll be fine," Azi re-assured me.

CHAPTER THREE

Carter and Azi set out on a journey to the dragon sanctuary.

After the diversion and distraction of the discussion on bush babies, we came back to discuss our goal which was how to accomplish our mission. Azi and I decided together on how to get to our destination. This was no longer fun for me because it was a serious talk not like the former. I started using my imagination to cook up ideas that would help. We were faced with two major questions. The first question was where would the sanctuary spot lie? The second was what route we were to follow to get there? I just remembered the third which was how Azi would avoid being seen by the evil people?

Trying to imagine a solution to these three questions became very difficult. It practically became a tug of war for us. The worst part was that I couldn't remember any story Grandpa told that could be of help. It was like an equation we both got stuck in. I just realized that this was more difficult than any of the chores mum usually asked me to do back home. Azi was completely clueless and when he eventually had something resembling an idea, it just ended up complicating our equation. Azi was in a melancholy state. He really looked pitiful and I felt sad for him. My hands were tied as we were both helpless. It was getting very late so we decided to find somewhere to sleep. It didn't take much time before we dozed off because we had a really exhausting day, plus we had no dinner.

I sort of had a sound sleep. I was so tired that the buzzing sounds of insects around weren't enough to stop me from sleeping. Azi was the first to wake up. He woke up distressed and hungry so he didn't hesitate to wake me up. I sluggishly woke up from the layer of leaves we slept on. After stretching and washing my face in a nearby stream, something sprang up within me. I just couldn't hold back a joyful smile with glee. Azi just stared at me in confusion and wondered what was wrong with me. I walked over so I could sit on a tree trunk. I beckoned Azi to come there also. I had a dream which dramatized one of Grandpa's stories. I just couldn't explain how I forgot this particular story from the previous day.

In that dream, I was a dragon in Grandpa's story. I had wings which enabled me fly high in the sky and human beings below stared up and waved to me. I flew across some landmarks before I got to the sanctuary land for dragons. As short as the dream was, that was it! The reason behind my smile didn't take me a minute to explain. Azi gave me a bewildering look and wondered if the dream was of any help. He asked how my barely minute long dream could solve our problems or take us to our destination. Reality dawned on me and I was able convince Azi. Azi was more than right! Before going on with the conversation, I begged Azi to give me some time to get him his breakfast.

After Azi was through with the plants I got for him, we resumed our great talk. Azi was not upset as he should have been because I solved the problem right on time. What was it? His breakfast! I knew he would have gotten upset after raising his hopes all for nothing. So, I decided to immediately get him something to eat in order to appease his cooking-up anger before it got done. On the other hand, I also felt bad because my evident joy at remembering the dream was because I thought the dream should have at least one answer to our questions. It's painful because my thought and feeling have never deceived me.

Azi saw the gloomy look on my face while he was eating. We resumed our conversation with that. He teased me by asking why I've not eaten and I smiled. He knew the answer because I told him during one of our friendly talks – I don't eat early. He then thought for a while then voiced out his thoughts. He told me to draw out any of the landmarks I could remember from the dream. This was easy for me because I liked drawing a lot.

As I began using a stick to draw on the sand, Azi watched my proposed drawing carefully and he gave me a look that was like he was seeing something that looked familiar. After some time, I was through and I was able to give an exact picture of the landmarks in my dream. Azi screamed in ecstasy because he could remember scene in the diagram clearly.

It was as if I handed over the baton to Azi. He was more than happy to take charge. I was more than happy as well because two of our questions had been answered. We now knew where we were going and what route to pass through.

"The third should eventually get an answer", I thought to myself.

How I was going to shield Azi from humans and Korvis who might still be after us became my major concern within a short time. I put my mind to rest with the unwavering faith that if we could find a solution to the two later questions, then we would surely find a lasting solution to the final quandary. Azi began to figure out what route would lead us out of where we were and onto our destination.

Azi indeed figured out a way. The end point of the tree trunk we sat upon earlier directly faced a bush path which obviously led somewhere. There were other bush paths around but this particular one was distinct. As Azi showed me the way, I had that inner conviction within me that we were on the right track.

Before setting off, I advised Azi that we should have something to eat before leaving since the journey was going to be a long one. Earlier Azi had told me that it was more than a day's journey. I was lucky to get some bugs for Azi while I plucked some fruit for myself. Immediately we were through eating and started off on our journey. There was no time for resting. If not, we would just sleep and that would mean lengthening our journey.

As we pressed on in this journey, we had this strange strength from within us. We moved with so much vitality. You know why? ...... we were going to reach our final destination soon enough and our mind will be at peace!

I began to tell Azi about my thoughts of being big and free from fear, threat, troubles and intimidations. I told Azi of how I thought that being big was the lasting road to freedom. With the little Azi and I have encountered, I realized that one's size wasn't a factor to the degree of one's problems. It was just something bond to happen, regardless of size. Azi smiled in confirmation and added that as big as he was, he wasn't entirely free from fear and challenges.

As we proceeded, we kept on engaging ourselves in funny conversation that amused us. We were so full of life as we marched forward like nothing could deter us any longer. We were so confident and weren't scared at all. We were so cocksure that we would get to our destination safely. Little did we know that our hope and assurance would soon be cut short.

We eventually landed on a strange farm that looked like it was close to a village. It was a rich farmland indeed, with all sorts of crops and vegetables. It looked like it had been deserted for a while based on the amount of the weeds surrounding it. We went there in search of food after tiring ourselves with long chit-chat talks.

Within in a short time, we settled on the farm like we were the owner or related to the owner. Azi began to help himself out with different vegetables he found. I was somehow unlucky because the things on the farm couldn't be eaten raw. I had to cook them before eating. I wished I was in Azi's shoes. I just sat on the floor watching Azi eat. Azi just looked away and pretended like he did not see me. He concentrated on eating like that day was going to be his last. His action gradually infuriated me. It was like he did not care about my wellbeing. The anger welling up inside me further increased my hunger. The sun was setting already.

As I watched Azi eating, I angrily hissed in my thoughts, not knowing it came out so loud in reality. Azi kept on giving me the silent treatment. Azi was only a foot long in size but ate like he was twice his size. He ate like there was no tomorrow. It made me boil that he was eating that much and I was not eating at all. Not exaggerating, he ate eighty percent of the vegetables on that farm like he was practically grazing. When he was finally through, I was eager to see his next line of action. I was rehearsing how I would angrily scream at him if he dared say we should continue the journey. I was anxious to hear his first sentence after his massive feeding.

When he finished eating to his satisfaction, he laid down to rest. After a while, he belched out loudly. It was so loud that someone miles away could hear him. It was not just the sound that caught my attention. I noticed smoke coming out of his mouth instead of just gas. I was astonished, but it did not last long because I was still angry at him. Moreso, I was eager to hear his words like a mother eager to hear her child's first words. He sat up and prepared to talk. I also sat up and prepared to give him an answer.

He asked, "What are you going to eat?"

I was shocked because these weren't any of the words I imagined him saying.

To be sure, I asked him to repeat what he said and he so did instead of me to give him a provoking reply. I decided to play along. I told him I wanted potatoes which were laying on one corner of the farm. He told me to bring it and I did so just to see the miracle he wanted to perform. He then told me to bring any pieces of dry sticks I could find around. I gave him a puzzling look before going to search for the sticks. He again told me to arrange the sticks like someone who wanted to roast. He finally told me to step aside. I stepped aside running out of ideas of what Azi wanted to do. To my utmost surprise, he spat out fire from his mouth!

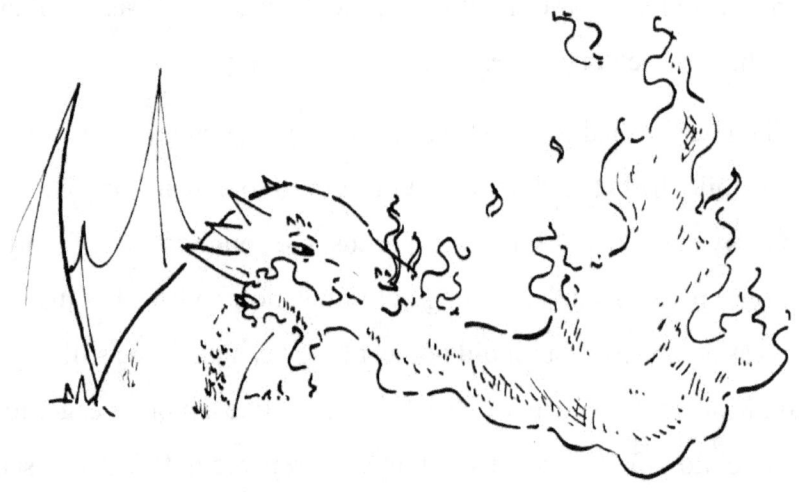

I was amazed and filled with awe. I knew some dragons spit out fire but never did I expect it from Azi. Apart from the fact that he was small in size and still growing, Azi just did not look like a fire-breathing dragon! I immediately roasted the potatoes, saving my questions for later. After roasting, I peeled off the back of the pota-toes and started eating while they were still hot. I hated cold food and didn't want to waste any more time. I ate hungrily and happily with passion. I roasted and ate ten big potatoes. I became really thirsty. Then I remembered that I saw a river while searching for sticks. I told Azi to there while I went to the river.

The location of the river looked farther than I thought. As I trekked on, I was whistling while remembering Azi's miracle. He really owed me a lot of explanation, I thought to myself.

"Why did he hide such a thing from me"? I asked myself.

As I walked to the bank of the river, I heard some sounds. At first, I was scared but I later realized it was the sound of bugs. I found a big stick not too far. So I held the stick as I tip-toed to where the bugs and hit them hard with the anger stored within me. The bugs died immediately. I put them aside as I went down to the river to have a drink. I drank to my satisfaction and filled the bottle I had with me.

As I put the bugs in a broad leaf I saw nearby, I began walking back to the spot I left Azi. I hummed a song Grandpa taught me while he was still alive. As I hummed with life in me, I didn't notice that a teardrop fell off my eye because of the memories of my Grandpa. I missed him deeply and it was like a part of me was gone. I immediately encouraged myself, recalling how nice and sweet Azi had been to me. He had been of immense help, and been a priceless

friend to me. He had proved to be a dependable and reliable friend…
he was a friend indeed. This encouragement got me going until I got
to the spot I left Azi. Lo and behold, Azi was nowhere to be found!

I searched everywhere on the farm, screaming out his name all to
no avail. I was confused and didn't know the next step to take. It was
as if my world came crushing down before my very eyes I slumped
on the floor, completely clueless on what had just happened.

"Could it be that the sweet dragon who saved my life and saved
me from hunger had been taken away by the evil one?" I repeatedly
asked myself.

I couldn't help it but my tears flowed freely. It was like my end
was staring fiercely at me. I put my hands akimbo echoing Azi's
name hoping for a miracle to happen since he was the miracle work-
er. Not long, I heard steps behind me with fright, I looked around and
found Azi laughing.

I screamed angrily at him because the prank he played wasn't a
funny one at all. I asked why he nearly made me insane with confusion. He laughed some more before apologizing for what he did. His
apology wasn't enough because I still had more questions to ask him.
He was surprised when I recalled the miracle he performed because
he thought I had forgotten about what happened. My memory was
still intact I told him. He then apologized again for not telling me he
could bring out fire from his mouth. He explained that he himself
wasn't sure he could do it since he was still in the growing stage. His

explanation was sincere.

He explained that he saw his father do it while he was still alive. According to him, Dara would eat a lot before spitting out fire. When he questioned the reason, Dara explained that emanating fire wasn't really part of his natural features. But he learned it. In order to do it, he had to eat more than his normal quantity because spattered out fire usually consume a lot of energy.

"So that was the trick I tried out earlier," Azi explained.

I saw his reasoning and understood why he was so caring that he didn't want to put my hopes up for nothing. Since he wasn't sure, I also recalled how I saw smoke come out of his mouth while he belched.

I then smiled at him but gave him two conditions before I would fully forgive him. I told him not to keep secrets from me again and never to play a costly and deadly prank on me. He agreed to my conditions and added that surprises could come up because he hadn't discovered himself fully yet. I told him I've heard him. He was about to say something when we suddenly saw someone approaching us. This was obviously a human being and I was overcome with fear and confusion on how to shield Azi.

The man yelled with authority, "Who are those on my farm?"

I was still trying to ask Azi what we could do when I realized it wasn't Azi that was with me but a human.

The figure I saw was a human looking like me. His facial appearance was akin to mine. I was dumbfounded and stricken with shock at yet another miracle I'd just seen. The figure whispered that he was Azi. I tried to calm myself with everything that just happened as the man was now standing in front of us. He began to interrogate us with different questions of what we were doing on his farm and how we got there. I started using my imagination to figure out a believable answer. We couldn't possibly tell him the truth as this would endanger our lives. So, I had to make up a story real fast.

I explained that we were from a village not too far from where we were. I also explained that we were orphans and twins. I added that ever since our parents died, we lived with a wicked uncle and his wife who continually maltreated us. So, we decided to run away from home. In search of our maternal grandmother whose village was some miles from where we were. I further added that it was due to hunger during our journey that we stopped on his farm in search of something to eat. The man looked at us with pity and forgave us trespassing on his land and offered to take us to his home.

The man looked like he was around my father's age. But facially older because his face was already wrinkling. We told him not to worry but he insisted though and appeared nice but I was scared that we couldn't trust anyone except ourselves. I then told the man that I needed consult with my brother first. Inclined to our request as we stepped aside and I asked Azi if he could remain human for long. Azi told me he could only last for forty-eight hours. He also added that it was only when in grave danger that he had such an ability. He added this to ease my mind that he wasn't intending to keep secrets from me.

I also asked if it would be comfortable for him to follow the man home. Azi said it was not a problem with him because he felt at ease with the man. He was also assured that the man wouldn't harm us. I smiled at him and told him how handsome he looked as a human. He smiled back then we proceeded to follow the man. The man was happy we accepted his request to offer help us. The man then asked why my twin was so quiet and I explained that it was just his nature. The man led the way and it didn't take us more than a few minutes to get to his home. His home was a portable looking hut.

His hut was the only one in the area. He lived in the outskirts of a small village. We asked him questions on why he was alone and far away from other villagers. By this time, it was getting late already. He insisted that he would provide us food to eat and water to drink before answering our questions. He was so warm and nice towards us. Azi and I were happy as we felt at home. It was like a home away from home. After we all were through eating, he began to provide answers to our question. He explained that ever since his wife died during child-birth he made up his mind to remain alone to honor her soul.

We felt bad for him on hearing the news. He added that it was as if his wife's spirit favored him. This was because everything he laid his hands upon prospered with little or no stress at all.

This explained why his land was so fruitful despite the fact that he rarely weeded the farm due to his poor sight. He couldn't see far and that was why he didn't see Azi as a dragon before he transformed into human form. I felt sorry for his sight problem but at the same time I was happy for Azi that he wasn't exposed. The man finally added the scary part. He said that there was a crazy man who insisted that was a dragon nearby, even though none had been found over the years.

At that moment, we trembled with fear because we could smell danger now. The man noticed how frightened we looked. He smiled and told us not to be scared because it was just a silly talk by the crazy fellow. According to him, he had never come across a dragon in all his years in that village, so we had nothing to fear. He chipped in the sweet part. He said that even if dragons existed, he was not of the belief that they were as dangerous or wicked as people think they are. Azi was so glad he found another human who didn't see dragons as wicked. He thanked the man. The man asked why. He jerked back to reality and said he was only thanking him for his hospitality.

After our long discussions, he led us to a room where we would rest for the night. The room was neatly prepared with a mat laid on the floor and a lit lantern like he was expecting visitors. We thanked him again in chorus before we laid down on the mat. I wondered to myself if it was his wife's spirit that also made the room purposely for us. As I looked at Azi, I made jest of his human form and tickled him. He kept on laughing and begging me to let him go. I later let him go and told him that that was punishment for all the stress he put me through. I could also confidently tell him that not all humans are bad as he could see for himself. We played some more before falling asleep.

We were so sound asleep that it was the good Samaritan who woke us up the next morning. We slept like babies. Azi quickly washed his face and it seemed like he was in a hurry. His limited time was the reason. The man insisted we had breakfast before leaving. We ate hurriedly, thanked the man with all our hearts before leaving. As we pressed on, we avoided the huts and passed through the bush instead. We then saw a vehicle moving and it excited me because I had been dying to see a moving vehicle. I only heard about one but never seen one. Azi shouted at me asking me why I was so happy. Azi was visibly upset. It was also then that I realized the ring in my finger began to glitter. Something was up!

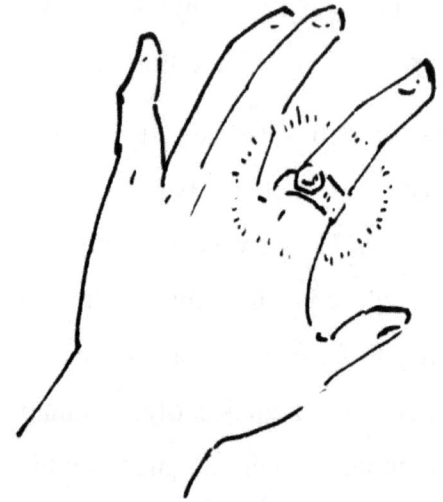

CHAPTER FOUR

Carter is captured by Korvis and Azi rescues him.

Azi eventually explained the reason for his anger to me since I couldn't understand his annoyance. He said that the vehicle we saw earlier was powered by dragon's blood. His senses could feel it so well as he had turned back to his real form already. It was this same reason that made my ring glitter so brightly because of its sensitivity. I now understood him perfectly but was scared that it seemed that danger lay ahead. I tried apologizing to Azi but he still seemed upset so. We continued our journey. It didn't take long before we got to the first landmark. Azi was the one who called my attention to that. I smiled because Azi's speculation was right. It was more than a day's journey.

We, in fact, got to the first landmark close to noon. By that time, we were already tired from the journey and we needed something to eat. We trekked to the nearby village which was just a stone's throw from the landmark. As we approached the village, we discovered that the village was a combination of medieval and industrial things. It also seemed like a combination of a rural and a developed area. I was surprised because I thought a village was supposed to be only one of the two. It looked amazing though. We also realized that the village appeared desolate. It looked like no one was around except for a few aged fellows we sighted some distance away.

Before taking the risk of being caught since it wasn't wise for Azi to turn into his human form yet, we retreated to hide in the bushes. As we stayed here, Azi found some bugs which he wasted no time in eating. Azi was always lucky in finding what he could eat faster than me. I just endured the hunger for those few moments because it was risky for me to leave him for anything in the world. He was like an amazing brother I never had from my biological parents. I had always wished for one but never imagined I would get one in this manner. It was sweet all the same though that a dragon turned to be my brother. I just smiled at him while he ate.

Looking at him eating reduced the hunger I felt because it was like a part of me was filled already. It was filled with an abstract kind of food and not the physical kind of food. As I looked afar, I discovered people started coming back into the village with items with them. It didn't take time for me to realize it was their market day. That explained why everywhere looked abandoned when we went there earlier. It seemed like a happy village filled with peace and unity. Looking afar behind the spot we stayed, I also noticed that there was another village there. It looked really smaller to the one we went earlier. Azi then advised we go to the smaller village to ask for direction to the other landmark.

I then asked Azi why we should go to the smaller village to ask for directions and not the bigger village. Azi explained that smaller villages were usually more abreast of their environment and landmarks than bigger villages. I was surprised and asked why it was so. He further explained that almost all of the residents in a small village were born there, thus, had a sound experience. On the other hand, those residing in bigger villages probably got there through migration. In other words, it was not their biological home town. I smiled at the sound knowledge and reason Azi had just passed on to me. I was glad inside that not only did I have a friend and brother with me, I also had a teacher.

As we began the journey to the smaller village, we found it took longer than what I expected on the way. I saw an almond tree and decided to pluck some fruit to eat before the hunger in me increase. The fruits I plucked were numbered about twelve. They were so sweet and I was glad I could not boast of being filled. Not long after this, we got to the village and Azi immediately transformed back into his human form. The villagers we saw around were quite a few. We decided to talk to the oldest since probably he would be more knowledgeable. He explained that the other landmarks could be located near the village we had just left. He wasn't sure of where it was exactly but knew that was the direction.

As we traveled back to the mixed-up village, I caught some fruit again while Azi helped himself with some more bugs. As we got closer, the sun set and flame lanterns came on all around the town but the flame is too red. Azi began to get upset again as my ring began to glitter. I asked Azi what the problem was this time and he explained that flame lanterns were also powered by dragon blood. At this moment, I also began to get angry. I wondered angrily why some humans had not one iota of regard for dragon life, like it was a mere chicken they could kill and eat. Finally, Azi and I were on the same side with regard to the anger issue.

It was getting late so I had to figure out a good interaction with the people so as to avoid suspicion. If we wanted to pass the night in this town, I really had to figure out something as soon as possible. I triggered my imagination to work because time was running out as one of the villagers now approached us. As he came nearer, I looked back at Azi now in human form. I didn't even realize when he transformed because I was so carried away by my thoughts. I thought to myself that if I came up with the story I told the good Samaritan, it wouldn't sound believable because these people were more exposed to the world and smarter.

They might begin to ask questions I would not be able to provide answers to. Also, they didn't look nice and sweet like the good Samaritan. I also thought that we could say we were researchers who wanted to do some research on their village. I was about settling on that make-up story when I realized it wasn't believable enough. Our ages would not match that of researchers. I also thought that we could say we had homework from school where we were told to study the villages around us. That also did not make much sense because we didn't look educated or like people who had ever gone to school in our entire life. I was beginning to get lost in thought when I remembered something.

I remembered that back in my village, actors were held with high esteem, whether children or adults. I didn't know if that would go over well with the people as a perfect explanation for our late presence in their town. I also figured that he didn't look well-off to be actors. The man finally asked us what we were doing in their town. I immediately replied that we were travelling children actors who were looking for somewhere suitable as a site for the location for our film. I also added that we were already in our costumes before realizing that our location was not exactly suitable. We wanted to go somewhere really sophisticated. The costume part in the story sufficed for our shabby look.

As I went on and on adding more flavor to my sweet make belief story, the man interrupted me. My heart pumped faster and faster. I was anxious to hear his next question. He told us that he wasn't interested in any further stories. He added that if we wanted to spend the night in their town, we had to work for it. He also chipped in that since it was late, he would allow us spend the night at the inn for free while we work for it the next day. I was surprised because it wasn't anything I expected. Azi and I were relieved because we were not questioned but were disappointed at the man's harsh treatment towards us. He wasn't even close to being hospitable.

He led us to the only inn in the town. While on his way to a room for us, he explained to the authorities that we were visitors on a journey who were going to pay the next morning by working it off. They nodded in agreement and let us in. The room wasn't exactly neat, but manageable for us to spend the night. I also asked the man if we could do extra work to pay for our food and he smiled nodded in agreement. The town people's hostility was greatly disheartening but we had no choice. He also added that there wasn't any food remaining for the night, so we should wait until the next day to get something to eat. Azi and I shook our heads in sadness. We had to spend the night without dinner.

As we lay on the not so clean mat in the room, which was barely large enough for us both, Azi sighed at the treatment of the man towards us. We both complained bitterly on how they were so unhospitable despite their exposure. In order to distract ourselves. Azi asked me how I could do what I did. I asked what it was. He then specified on how I could be so fast in imagining things and making up stories. I just smiled and told him it was amazing that it was just a talent because he felt I had to study thoroughly to be able to imagine as well as I did. I began feeling like I was some boss.

Azi just laughed at how I could still make light of the whole situation we found ourselves in. I was still feeling good about myself when Azi began to tickle me. It was now his turn; what goes around, comes back around. I begged him to stop after laughing uncontrollably that he finally did. I later added that it was one of my dreams to become an actor. Because I just loved the features of the profession. Azi exclaimed and now realized why it was so easy and simple for me to come up with a make belief story and act it out so well. I was prompt in switching to any kind of character. Our talk drove away the thunder we felt. It didn't take time before we eventually fell off to a much needed sleep.

We woke up on our own without any help. Azi was the first to awaken. He yawned loudly and stretched his body. It was dawn already. So, he woke me up. It took a while after Azi hit me before my eyes were finally awake. Azi was upset at how long it took me to fully wake up. He was surprised because I wasn't a heavy sleeper. I apologized to him and explained that it was a dream I had that delayed my waking up. Azi was anxious to know the details of the dream. I didn't tell him immediately because I wanted to punish him for being so mean in hitting me to tell him. It was now my turn.

I let it go after a while. Before telling him the dream, I looked through the window and realized how quiet everywhere was. It was like we were the only ones awake. I now observed that the town's people were lazy. Judging from their going to the market by noon instead of in the morning, their long sleep and their wanting us to work for them, it was more than obvious. I just sighed and sat down to finally tell Azi my dream. In the dream, the next landmark was revealed to me. In the dream, I also learned that it can be reached by crossing a big river at the bridge in Cerra which is a large town. I've already had heard about it. Again, it was going to be more than a day's journey.

Azi was happy and relieved that we were making progress. It

seemed God was on our side. I also smiled in affirmation. We now started discussing what kind of work we would be asked to do. We were really hungry now and we would have no choice but to do whatever kind of work we would be given. Our discussion was interrupted by a loud knock on our door. Finally, someone else was awake! We told him to come in aid he did so. The man seemed to be like the care-taker of the inn. He was one and the same with the man we met yesterday who led us to the inn. It was obvious he forced himself out of a restful sleep based the way he kept yawing after entering our room.

He managed to greet us good morning. He then told us we were to wash the dishes from the previous day for spending the night. My mouth opened in annoyance while Azi just shook his head. We agreed since we didn't have much of a choice. Azi then asked what work we would be doing to pay for our breakfast. The man told us to take one step at a time, that he would tell us after we were through eating. In other words, after the first work detail, we would eat and wait until the next work detail. We reluctantly followed him as he led us to the inn's kitchen. The dishes were in six different piles and each was so telling. We shared and shouted in anger.

We had to ask if it was all we were going to wash and the man nodded in affirmation. It was as if they piled them in expectation of us. We had no choice, so, we started off immediately as the man left us. Our hunger was already increasing, so we had to be fast. After a while, we finally finished the dishes. The man came around at about that time and was surprised at how fast we were. He then smiled and led us to the restaurant of the inn. He led us to a seat where we sat awaiting food. We were given boiled potatoes with palm oil. At least the food was worth it. As we were eating, some other people walked into the restaurant. We heard them say something that caught our attention.

We overheard their conversation which made us shake with fear. They said that there was a scarcity of the fuel they made from dragon's blood. Azi simmered slowly but managed to keep his temper as I tried to calm him down. I could see Azi's face raging with anger. It was really annoying for me also, but it wasn't up to that of Azi. He knew where the nail pinched him the most. I was still trying to assure Azi that everything will be fine when someone walked in with some followers. When I looked to see who it was, it was our beloved Korvis. It was as if we were caught unaware. I likened it to that moment when one's enemy finally catches up to you.

I just held on to Azi's hands, convincing him that he should keep calm. I knew it wasn't going to be easy for him. I assured Azi that Korvis didn't recognize him as a human, so he was safe. Our last encounter with him was so sudden, thus, it wasn't possible for him to recognize us. I just advised that we keep low a low profile for the meantime. As Korvis sat down with his other dragon hunter followers, they began laughing and boasting of all their successful dragon kills. This got Azi madder and madder and I was scared that Azi was going to lose his control and do something stupid. To make it worse, we were told to perform instead of washing dishes to pay for our meal.

Trying to calm myself, I figured I was going to use my imagination to tell a fantastic story. Before I knew what was happening, Azi climbed up the stage! I could smell a lot of trouble coming up. He wanted to tell a story instead, even though he hadn't consulted with me. Azi stepped up onto stage to tell a story. His story was about a dragon and human born on the same day. They were able to do amazing things together. The audience was spell bound. But as Azi's control slipped, he reached the part where the dragon is injured and dies. The human also dies of a broken heart. Before the crowd could see hints of a dragon under the illusion, Korvis and other hunters got the picture. They rushed at Azi.

Before they could get to Azi, I quickly managed to trip them giving Azi enough time to escape. Since Azi and I looked alike, the hunters were confused. As such, Azi was able to escape. I was also trying to escape. Then they caught up with me and held me hostage. I was now in the Lion's den! I hoped for the best because I was now in the hands of the mighty! How would I be rescued? Who would come to my aid? Was this really the end for me? The questions kept on popping into my mind. I couldn't even hope that the town's people would help out because they were all on Korvis' side. The only thing that gave me joy was that Azi was safe.

Even if I would be killed, I would die a happy man because I was able to save a friend, brother and teacher. It was indeed worthwhile. I was first of all tortured with some instruments. It was during the process of my being torturing that they realized I was not a dragon. All the while, they thought Azi and I were both dragons because of the fact that we both looked alike. They were surprised that a young human like myself would give himself up to be tortured for a dragon. Anyways, that did not deter the progress of their plan. They stopped their torture and changed the concept of their plan to capture the real dragon who was Azi! I became more distressed over that.

It was enough that they were torturing me and left me in pain. I got angry that they would be asking for too much by wanting to capture Azi. After finding out I wasn't a dragon, they tied me up in a shed at the back of the inn's yard while they stood guard. I now figured out their new plan. They wanted to use me as bait to capture Azi. I was frustrated by this because I knew Azi would fall for it. I was still happy to some extent that I was the only one in their custody. It would make me go crazy if they also captured Azi. At least I was still alive though in pain. If they captured Azi, his life would be the first thing they would take from him.

After they settled this, they set off to refine their plan and left me in pain. I was raving mad with thoughts of they were about to do to Azi. I just had to find a way out to help my friend. While alone, I began to think of a way to escape. I then remembered that I still had my grandfather's pocket knife with me. I searched my pocket with some difficulty but eventually found it there. I was extremely happy. As I managed to work it out of my pocket, I heard a commotion outside and decided to make a break for it. With lots of struggle and pain, I used the knife to cut the rope around me. I finally succeeded and ran out. I tip toed when I got outside Korvis' yard. As I ran again, I ran into Korvis himself!

I was in between the devil and the deep blue sea. I was face-to-face with the devil. Trying to run back, the remaining hunters were right behind me. I was cocksure this was the end of the road for me. Korvis began to laugh hysterically at me. The same went for other hunters. I had even forgotten I had a knife with me that could be of immense help. I now believed that in time of fear, one could forget his name. The pains of the torture came back to me. It was like I was being tortured all over again. I trembled with fear as I knelt down to beg for their mercy. I knew they wouldn't budge but that was the only option I saw for me.

The funny thing was that I wasn't begging for my life. I was begging that they wouldn't harm my friend, Azi. This infuriated Korvis and he swung his knife at me. That was just one of the weapons he had on him. As his knife got to me, it cut my side. I fell flat on the ground as the cut was really deep. I held my side and cried out in pain. It was as if my life was being drained before my very eyes. Korvis shouted in victory and said that that just a warning. According to him, anyone that came in his way in his bid for hunting dragons will pay with his dear life. There's a sudden roar as a dragon appeared. The dragon attacked and rescued me. It was Azi!

It all looked like magic to me. Azi immediately picked me up and carried me away. I felt so loved and happy that Azi could do all that for me. He didn't fly that high before he had to land at a nearby bush. We managed to get away, but I was still bleeding and wriggling in pain because of the deep injury. Azi placed me on the ground. He breathed fire on the wound and healed it. I immediately felt much better. I kept on thanking him for what he had done. He told me not to thank him because he should be the one thanking me for taking such a deadly risk for him.

All in all, we both helped each other. So I deserved his thanks and he deserved my thanks. He still insisted I should rest because I wasn't fully fit. I reluctantly obliged his request even though I felt much better and stronger. The fire Azi breathed and my blood combined into a stone similar to the one in my finger which my grandfather gave me. Azi handed it over to me. He told me to never to lose it because it had the strength of both humans and dragons. He further explained that it was stronger than the one I had on my finger. I took it from him and would keep it somewhere safe. I thanked him again.

I was so pleased with him that I gave him a hug. Azi also smiled at me. He also apologized for not telling me he could fly. I interrupted him adding that I understood perfectly. His ability to fly was still a work-in-progress because he couldn't fly so high. He smiled at the way I could understand him so well. We barely had time to rest and bond properly when the sounds and commotion of the dragon hunters appeared nearer. We prepared to start moving again. Our move had to be very fast so that our enemies wouldn't catch up with us. We headed back to the countryside, finally managing to lose our pursuers. As we got there, we were both so exhausted that we readily went to sleep.

CHAPTER FIVE

Carter and Azi Meet Yamina

The hot chase by the hunters gave Carter and Azi was so much that being "exhausted" was an understatement. They were just wanting to sleep it off. They found some palm fronds at the edge of the countryside. It was after much panting that they decided to rest there for the night. They were more than exhausted to start looking for water to drink even though they needed it dearly. They were not only thirsty. They were hungry as well because the last meal they ate was their breakfast. Time was fast spent and it was really getting dark. It would have been dangerous and a big risk on their part if they decided to start looking for something to eat and drink considering all they'd been through. They didn't have second thoughts about sleeping there for the night and finding a solution to their predicament the next morning.

It couldn't have been called a sweet sleep because their sleep was far from being sweet. They couldn't sleep with both eyes closed. Being alert was at the center of both of their minds. The best adjective to describe what they had would be "rest" or "siesta." These words would have been appropriate. The next morning, they woke up feeling so weak and drained because of the previous day's experience. There weren't any dreams as expected. They desperately needed to look for water to drink and food to eat hopefully before continuing on their journey.

Luckily for them, there was a stream not too far from where they were. Carter was the first to see it. It looked like in addition to the gift of imagination, he also had the gift of seeing far away like wolves and eagles. This totally impressed Azi especially when it met his needs. Carter led the way and Azi followed. It was as if God was always on their side. They were favored, reason being that they always found water close by no matter how desolate the area they found themselves in.

It wasn't long before they got to the stream. It was a really big stream and could be akin to a river. With the way it looked, it was probably the source of water for all of the countryside. They were lucky that the towns people didn't wake up early enough to meet them. They faced their mission there and drank water to their satisfaction.

They were so filled with water that it took a while before they thought of what to eat. Their efforts to find something to eat proved abortive as their search in the area was in vain and to no avail. Azi became so affected that he couldn't get anything to eat. Neither bugs nor vegetables could be found anywhere. It was painful for them both because they had missed both lunch and dinner the previous day. Now, they were about to miss breakfast as well. Carter deeply thought of what to do but found next to no answers at all. Carter encouraged Azi that they should move on with their journey to Cerra further put a ray of light of hope on Azi that they could find what to eat on their way.

Azi reluctantly agreed to Carter's advice because he obviously didn't have a better idea or choice himself. As they began their journey in a weary state, their movement could be equated to that of a snail. Carter assuming the post of a big brother decided to make light the whole situation. He remembered his grandfather saying that he should always learn to see the brighter side to every situation he would find himself in. As he remembered, it was like his grandfather envisaged such a day like this one he was stuck into. Not too long after Carter's brisk thought, he remembered a joke his grandfather told him. He gathered all the strength left in him and began the joke. In the joke, there was a boy who always got beaten by his father due to the intrusion by the father's friend who came visiting often. On this day, the father's friend came as usual but the boy's father was absent. The boy explained that his father had gone to the farm but would soon be back. The man decided to wait. The boy began consuming sweets his mother bought for him from the neighboring town. After the boy ate eight wraps, the man started intruding as his usual style. He told the boy to stop eating it because he could die. The boy exclaimed and decided to teach the man the lesson of his life. The boy replied that his grandfather lived for 150 years and he lived that long because he always minded his own business.

Azi jerked back to life with so much laughter. He persistently laughed all through five minutes following the end of the joke. Carter had never seen Azi laugh that much that he too also laughed in amazement. He laughed with joy that he could put joy on Azi's face.

Azi began to make comments on the joke after he managed to end his round of laughter. He commented that it really served the man right since he was a busybody who liked interfering in other people's matters. He explained that it was sheer joblessness that made people leave their own home and go to someone else's house just to make a show off of intrusion with stupidity. The use of Azi's grammar also made Carter burst into laughter. Carter also affirmed what Azi said. He added that the man's assumption of death from licking sweets was absolutely wrong. He explained that his grandfather told him that too many sweets only decayed teeth and nothing more. This distraction helped them forget their troubles for a while.

As they trekked on further, they both realize the journey to Cerra was more than they thought. After a mile's trek, they found the answer to their proposed lunch since they had missed as he found both already. Azi had double blessings as he found both bugs and vegetables at the same time. Carter also helped himself with some fruit he found around. They ate their fill and became more serious with their journey as they finally reached the countryside.

Cerra was the biggest town they had seen so far. It could be akin to paradise compared to all other villages and towns they had seen so far. No one notices them at first because of the hustle and bustle of the town. They notice more machines than mechanical things. It looked so cool to Carter. Not long after looking around the town, Carter noticed Azi was upset. He also noticed that the stone Azi gave him began to glow endlessly. Without further ado, Carter got the clear message. Most machines in Cerra were powered by dragon blood. Carter tried to calm an upset and sad Azi because anger was one of the most difficult tasks Carter had faced so far. This was because it never worked out well. It always ended up in a tragedy or mess. At this moment, Carter began to perceive trouble coming ahead. He knew Azi's anger won't end well for them. Disaster could well be the end of the whole drama. Carter advised Azi to transform into human form to avoid any more trouble. It would also help to deter any suspicions or greater risks. They were now in the midst of people but no one questioned them. They were too many in the village for anyone to have noticed someone different. It was as if they were in a market square. Carter urges Azi to keep moving toward the bridge in order to cross it to get to the next landmark.

Everyone in the village was going about with their own different activities that no one talked to Carter and Azi. Though Carter urged Azi to move to the bridge, the irony was that they neither one knew where the bridge was.

Azi had an idea of where it might be but wasn't sure. They both decided to ask around amidst the hustle and bustle of the town. As they kept on talking to people to ask for direction, no one gave them a listening ear. They were absolutely ignored as no one had the spare-time for chi-chat. It was obvious that the town's people were hardworking and diligent. They were all busy and productive in their endeavors.

Though the people were busy and hardworking, they weren't accommodating or nice at all. They were just too hostile towards the duo. Carter and Azi decided to rest for a while when Azi reminded Carter of something. Azi made Carter realize that the stream they saw earlier wasn't the source of water for Cerra as Carter had suggested. This is because Azi sees a well around where some of the people were fetching from. Carter agreed with Azi and accepted the correction. He realized Azi was right considering how far the stream was from the town. They eventually saw someone who was about to listen to them when Carter sighted Korvis in the crowd. The need to keep going got stronger.

"Korvis wouldn't just give in, would he?" Carter thought to himself.

Carter told Azi that if Korvis was that determined to get them, they also should not rest on their Loral's. The desire to not give up had been injected into Azi. They still approached the person who wanted to listen to them and hopefully help out. They intended to use the man as cover to lose track of Korvis. Korvis hadn't sighted them yet so it was easy for them to plan ahead.

"It is always good to take advantage of the upper hand you have against your enemy before he can strike," Azi thought aloud.

As they approached the man, they were lost on what they wanted to ask him. They were so restless and unsettled. The man had to ask them what the problem was because they were speechless. Carter was so far in thought that Azi was the one who spoke. Azi's mind was also in disarray and didn't know when he asked the young man that if it was the way to the market they were looking for. The man realized they were stranger's and addressed them with courtesy. He warmly welcomed them and explained that the market was a stone's throw from where they were standing. He was trying to give a detailed direction when Azi was jerked back to reality. He was surprised to have been hearing stuff about the market when Korvis was in the real sense their major problem, plus getting to know where the bridge was in order to get to the next landmark. Azi was also lost as he realized he asked the wrong question. Before they could remedy the situation, the unexpected happened.

Korvis sighted them and made his way out of the crowd to give the duo a chase. The two abandoned the homely young man and began to run as fast as their legs could carry them. They ran like they were competing for the medal of the millennium. Korvis was the only one giving chase. It was like his hunters were not with him this time around. Looking at it from another angle, it was possible they were just hanging around elsewhere. They probably spread themselves around in order to make the capture easier. Whichever way, they were in a great deal of trouble. It was as if trouble itself decided to stick with them come rain or come shine. Some of the town's people just stayed back to watch like it was some drama unfolding before their very eyes. Some just went about doing their work. They were so indifferent like it wasn't a life that was at stake. Only a few seemed really concerned about the whole saga. They looked bothered and were trying to ask others if they knew what the issue was. If only these few knew that it was a life or two that was on the line, they would have probably come to the duo's rescue. The hot chase continued and was obvious that neither of the three relented in their energetic race. The big question was who would be the winner? It was like a race to check the survival of the fittest. Who was going to survivor? Was it Carter who was running with his gigantic height and muscles or Carter or Azi who was running with his legs scattered? Azi wasn't used to running with legs.

Among the three supposed athletes, Azi was the first to get tired

and exhausted. When Carter realized that Azi was now losing him
and that the gap within them was getting broader, he decided to go
back to assist his friend. Carter tried holding unto Azi's hands so that
the race could continue. Due to the delay created by Azi, Korvis was
gradually getting closer to the two. Carter tried encouraging Azi but

he was already growing weary. He kept on complaining that he
wanted to rest despite the fact that Korvis was about to catch up with

them. Carter didn't know how to explain to a weak Azi that he
shouldn't care about his present tiredness, so far his life was still intact. Carter did not know how angry he was getting until he barked at
Azi asking him if that was how he was going to avenge Dara's death!

As if that was not enough, Carter added that, "if your life means nothing to you, it means more than a lot to me."

No sooner had Carter finished his statement than Azi gave an impressive run with anger and vibe. It was like Carter injected Azi with a great height and passion. Even Carter had to increase his pace of running before he could catch up with Azi. Carter stared at Azi's face and could read anger, provocation and, most importantly, determination. In their bid of running they ran through peoples' compounds and at a point, ran in circles. The race is now falling in favor of Carter and Azi. They began to lose Korvis far behind them. Not long after, something strange happened.

Realizing they had given Korvis a lot of gap and probably lost him, the duo decided to take a minutes' rest. They leaned on a hut nearby which had a well in front. The well was jam-packed with different women fetching water for their home. Water was a dire need for the duo but they were too weak to ask for water. As if God heard their heart desires, one of the women approached them and offered them water to drink. They drank like never before. They drank so much water, like people who were just released from a desert after a week. After drinking water, they thanked the woman for her kindness. She left them and went back to her work.

Carter seized the opportunity to quickly apologize for his harsh words earlier. Azi accepted the apology with maturity accepting that what Carter said was the bitter truth. Although painful he thanked Carter for placing so much value on his life, even more than he did himself. Carter was happy that Azi received everything calmly. He then advised that they look for somewhere to hide before continuing their race. Azi suggested they ask the woman who offered them water for help since she seemed nice. Before they could make or stick to a conclusion, the unexpected happened again.

Korvis was already close by and was gradually approaching them. After they resumed their running for some minutes, a vehicle stops in front of them. The driver, who happened to be a girl, urged them to come in. Azi vehemently warned Carter that it could be a trap and it would be better if they continued running.

Carter, on the other hand, sincerely felt they should give in to the girl's kind gesture. Azi didn't go down well with that. He just felt trusting her was not a good idea. Carter advised that it was best they enter the vehicle since Korvis was really getting nearer. Azi is reluctant but when Carter realizes Korvis was getting really closer, he is left with no better choice than to enter. They both entered and the car zoomed off with great speed. Korvis got there almost immediately and bit his finger in regret that he lost his prey. He wasn't with a vehicle at hand but pursuing the speeding car on foot wouldn't have been a wise idea. He shook his head in annoyance and gave that look of 'the battle is not over yet.'

Giving up on his victims was never in Korvis' dictionary. Korvis' level of determination, persistence and resolution were worthy of commendation. Azi's heart was beating real fast like he was in for greater trouble. Since they both sat in the backseat of the vehicle, it was easy for Carter to calm Azi down. There was a dead silence amongst the three of them in the car. No one knew what precise things to say. Carter and Azi just communicated with blind gesticulations. It was as if there were deaf and dumb people in the vehicle. Carter eventually broke the silence as he thanked the girl for coming to their rescue and, helping them out at the time of dire need. The girl just smiled and told them it was her pleasure. Azi also spoke out and demanded to know how she could drive so well considering the fact that she was a female.

It was his curiosity that made him ask that. It wasn't like he really cared about a girl driving. He felt he could push words out of her mouth and made her confess who she really was. His major concern was if she was also part of the enemy is camp sent to entrap them. He wanted to know if it was a safe haven or a pit in paradise. She answered and said she learned it from her father who taught her extensively while he was still alive. Carter immediately interrupted and said they were sorry about her father's death. He felt pity for her as he couldn't imagine losing his father after his Grandpa's death. She accepted his sympathy but added that it was nothing, since she was over the whole thing already. Carter was shocked to hear that statement. It was as if she released a bombshell. Could it be that his Grandpa he thought was dead was actually alive somewhere? How come the girl in question knew her Grandpa? Why did the girl face him with the question and not Azi? These questions came rushing through Carter's mind. All Azi could think of was suspicion. He was so sure the girl was asked strange and weird questions and, as such, she should be avoided. The girl's questions looked like she was avoiding something. The girl's questions looked like she was up to no good but to do mischief. Carter was still in a state of shock and could not bring himself to answer the girl's question about his Grandpa. Another principal question that came to Carter's mind was, "Who was the girl?" Her identity was the key to answer other questions.

Puzzling enough, the girl did not pester them with the question. She only asked once and kept mute. She drove on like nothing transpired between them at all. They finally pulled off at the front of a really nice house. Azi was still pensive as he thought about who owed the house and why she pulled off there. Carter on the other hand was so lost in thought that he didn't realize the speeding car had already come to a halt. After parking under a shade tree, she highlighted from the car and told them to come out of the car and follow her. It was so sure that it was just Azi who heard her since Carter was still sitting comfortably. Azi was coming out of the car when he realized Carter didn't even move an inch. He went back to tap Carter back to life and told him to come down.

Carter journey back to the word of reality from the world of imaginations. He got down from the car and followed Azi on the led the way to the house. As they got to the house, she was coming back out as they went in to relax from the race and long speedy journey. They began to look around the house. It was a beautiful one with lots of pictures hung around the wall. Some of the pictures were those of dragons. There pictures were a surprise to them. They thought of reasons why she should have pictures of dragons in her home. Unending questions kept popping-up in their minds.

Not long after, she came out and offered them food to eat and water to drink. Despite their doubts, they couldn't ignore the food they were offered. They ate to their satisfaction and thanked her. Their meal could be best described as a nutritional and satisfying lunch. It was far more than refreshments even thought that was what she called it. She also joined them in the meal before sitting in the parlor to relax with them and prepare for a long discussion; the discussion was inevitable because they all had lots of issues to iron out amongst themselves. Their meal was a quick one because silence was the order of the hour. Carter was the first to break the silence as he asked the girl how she knew his grandfather. She started by explaining her identify. She s explains that her name was Yamina and she was a student of Grandpa. According to her, he had not only taught her history, literature and mathematics, but also the folklore of dragons that most people had forgotten. Azi and Carter looked on in amazement hoping to hear more surprises. It was at this hoping to hear more surprises that Carter realized he really didn't know much about his grandfather like he thought he did. Neither his mother, father nor Grandpa himself ever mentioned that he had once been a teacher. All Crater could remember was that there was a period Grandpa travelled but he didn't tell him where he was going. All his Grandpa told him was that he was going for an important trip which meant a lot to him.

Azi too was shocked at the turnout of the whole event since he never heard from both Dara and Carter himself the whole story Yamina was now talking about. On the other hand, there was another part of Azi who chose not to believe Yamina's story. That part of Azi felt that Yamina could be making up the whole story. Azi was filled with the fear of the unknown and was totally confused on what to believe and what not to believe. Carter was still blank with all he heard from Yamina. It just didn't add up or make any sense to Carter. This was because he wondered and tried to imagine reasons why his grandfather would have hidden something like that from his whole family. He also wondered if that was the reason why his grandfather could probably be alive.

Although there was no link at this point, he just felt anything could be possible. A little part of him still felt that all Yamina's actions could be a trap; his mind was in disarray which was to be expected. Yamina went ahead with her confusing story.

According to her, Carter's Grandpa had told her he had to travel but before he left, he gave her a necklace. She abruptly paused her conversation and went to her window to check if anyone was peeping in or ease dropping on their conversation. This was funny because her house was the only one in the area. They crossed the almighty bridge before getting to her home. Her house could be likened to the only tree in a desert. Before the duos died from suspense, Yamina came back with more confidence and decided to continue her story.

As she continued, she added that Carter's Grandpa had also told her that if the necklace ever shone, she'll know he was back. when the necklace started humming, she'd gone to find him but found Carter and Azi instead. According to Yamina, she had been to several villages in search of Grandpa after he left. Though the necklace didn't hum, she searched all over for him because she missed him and wanted him back as her teacher. No one had taught her so well like Grandpa did. The little time he spent with her meant so much to her. Grandpa was able to deposit more than a lot in Yamina within the little time he spent with her. Her mother also encouraged her to look for him seeing that he had done a lot of good in her daughter's life. Ever since Yamina's father passed away, it was only Grandpa who could put her to order and controlled her unruly and carefree nature. Grandpa became like a second father to her. Her mother was so fed up with her and left her to her ways. She did whatever she liked and anyhow, she liked it while her mum just ignored her because she didn't know what else to do. She was practically fed up with reprimanding her daughter with little or no results. All her efforts to give her daughter a better life was to no avail. Eventually, her prayers to make her daughter a better person were answered with the great arrival of Grandpa into their lives.

Her grades in school were deteriorating really badly. The death of her father made her a mess. The only man she ever loved and respected was snatched away from her by the shackles of death. The painful part was that he died mysteriously. His dead body was found on the farm without any injuries or cuts. His death was unexplainable until the very moment she was discussing with Azi and Carter. The pain was too much for young Yamina to bear. She was five years old at that time. Her childhood had been brutally traumatized by the sudden death of her father. She was really close to her dad and it was as if the great bond she had with him had been broken. It was akin to a piece of her heart being snatched away from her. It wasn't just a piece but an important piece. She wasn't really close to her mother because she was always busy in the library where she worked. It was only in the evenings that she spent quality time with her mum. Her father was a successful farmer whose plants yielded bountifully at every harvest period. The family was pretty close to being wealthy. It also helped matters that they had just one child, which was Yamina. Grandpa came as a stranger to their town and offered to be a personal teacher to Yamina in order to teach her during the holiday. Her mother embraced the opportunity since Yamina's grades were going bad.

Yamina's mum didn't mind that he was a stranger since she was in dire need of Yamina's life to come back on track. Since he was an old man, she felt he was going to be really experienced and, as such, be able to handle Yamina. It was like an opportunity she couldn't miss for anything in the world. Grandpa did not disappoint her as he met all her expectations. He was able to mold Yamina into the perfect daughter she had always dreamed of. He handled her so well with so much understanding that she grew up to be a mature young girl. What he taught her became a foundation for remaining years as she grew up. He spent just a year with them and he had already become an integral part of their lives. He was living with them through the whole year. Yamina could be very rude to her mother, but not to Grandpa because she still had some respect for him since he was an

old man. He never traded words with her. Rather he treated her calmly and wisely with a lot of maturity. As Yamina's mum thought, he
was indeed an aged man with a lot of experience. It didn't take much
time before she amended her ways and turned over a new leaf. Her
mentality had been changed positively and she now saw or viewed
life in a different dimension. It was now obvious to her mum that fire
could never quench fire. Only water could do that job perfectly. The
patient dog indeed ate the fattest bone. Although, in his case, it
wasn't the dog. Yamina's grades were now better and she always
emerged on top in her class.

It was at this juncture Yamina had to pause her story because
Carter was already in tears while Azi's eyes were also red. Carter
began to miss his Grandpa all over again. The way he missed him
was beyond what words could comprehend. Here, the boys decided
to take over as Carter offered to explain his Grandpa's death. It had

been almost a year since his Grandpa died. Just like the death of Yamina's father, Grandpa died mysteriously. Although many attributed it to old age, it was still unexplainable to Carter because Grandpa was fully fit, agile and full of life. Unlike Yamina's dad, Grandpa didn't live with Carter. He lived in the neighboring village even though it seemed strange. Carter's parents usually took Carter along to visit his Grandpa once in a while. He, on the other hand, went to visit his father often on his own but with his parent's permission. It was like his second home. He even slept over most times because he felt his Grandpa would be lonely sleeping all alone. Until the present moment, he didn't understand why they had to live separately. To Carter, it was uncalled for because it wasn't like they didn't have an extra room where Grandpa could lay his head. Carter's recurrent thought was that his parents were hiding something from him because they felt he was too young to understand or digest. He couldn't argue with his parents too much because to them, he would always remain a young lad who could never grow up.

Grandpa was the only one who could fathom his dragonish beliefs and imagination Even his mum and dad could never see reason with his crazy imaginations and beliefs. When his Grandpa was still alive, a lot of people around the village usually laughed at him. To some, old age was responsible for his crazy beliefs and actions which Carter inherited from him. To others, they believed that Carter's Grandpa was probably retarded mentally. These comments and jest usually annoyed Carter. It got him angry that the people were mocking the only man who understood him perfectly. Grandpa always saw a lot of sense in whatever Carter said, especially when it related to his imagination. It was even Grandpa who told Carter that he had the gift of imaginations. He told him never to give up on exercising the great gift he had. So far, he was glad he heeded Grandpa's advice because it had indeed helped him a great deal. When Grandpa died, Carter cried uncontrollably for days because he had lost a legend in his life. To Carter, Grandpa was not just an old man. He was a father, mother, teacher, friend, confidant or any proper adjective that could deeply explain what someone special depicted. Grandpa was unforgettable, irreplaceable, nonexchangeable and irrevocable to Carter. It was no more than a shock to Carter that after the period of Grandpa's death, Grandpa was in fact still alive for the one year he spent with Yamina. This hurt Carter.

Deciding to stop talking about Grandpa's death at this point, the boys also explained a little about their journey so far but do not reveal Azi's true form. Azi adds that he is a close friend of Carter. He explains and lies that he and Carter have been childhood friends. He also said that after the supposed death of his Grandpa, Carter suggested that they went for an adventure to look for the dragon sanctuary. This was because Carter was still very upset with his dragon beliefs. Azi chipped in that because of their tight friendship, he offered to follow Carter on his journey so that Carter could use it as an opportunity to forget his sorrows. It would be a distraction for them both and they could put their youthful energy to good use. During Azi's telling of the story, Carter just shook his head in disbelief that Azi could use his imaginations really well. He smiled thereafter to himself happily and with lots of pride. The reason was obviously because he felt he was becoming a good, just like his Grandpa. Azi continued his story by adding that in the course of their journey, they had met all sorts of people. According to him, they had come across a few hospitable and homely people and some very hostile ones as well. It was there that Carter interrupted him with the adage that said there were only but a few good men were overly correct. Azi further explained by saying who Korvis was.

Azi also lied again because of the distrust he still had for Yamina despite all she had said so far. He said that when they got to Cerra, the man whose name they heard was Korvis started pursuing them seriously. The reason being that he was a dragon hunter who thought them to be dragons because of how well they narrated dragged stories. Before they could explain themselves, Korvis began to give them a hot chase like he had seen meat for supper he didn't want to let go. It was during this race for their lives that Yamina picked them up. Carter just opened his eyes in amazement because of Azi's well cooked up lies. He understood the real reason behind Azi's lies, which was fear of the unknown coupled with the fact that he had no faith whatsoever in Yamina. Yamina looked at the boys with pity because of the tragic story they shared with her. She felt really bad about Carter's Grandpa's death and the mystery about his being alive after his supposed death. She felt guilty because it looked like she stole the little time Carter could have spent with his Grandpa. She expressed her sadness, sympathy and condolences in deep words. They all decided to leave the complicated part of Grandpa's death. Not long after, Azi concluded that he and Carter were to leave soon. Yamina offered and insisted they spent the night at her house before continuing their journey.

Azi reluctantly stayed back as Carter tried to encourage him and cheer him up with all sorts of gesticulations. Yamina led them to the bathroom where they got cleaned up. While they were cleaning up, Yamina made their supper in the kitchen. After they were through cleaning up, she beckoned to them to join her for dinner. For the first time after a long while, the boys ate with joy, gladness and peace of mind like they were in a safe haven. As they all ate happily, Yamina offered to tell them about the lore of dragons and humans that Grandpa had once told her. According to her, the lore involved how humans and dragons worked together in harmony in the past. The boys were eager to listen since it related to dragons. Azi was finally having some confidence in Yakima. Carter was relieved for Azi since his fear would now be put to rest. She continued her folklore by adding that the harmony continued until humans discovered that they could harness the power of dragon blood to run their machines effectively and faster. From then on, dragons were hunted and the bonds between the duo were broken. The boys acted so well by giving a sigh of pity for the dragons in the story though Azi remembered that it was similar to the story of Joe that Carter told him, he still pretended like he was hearing the story for the first time.

Going further, Yamina said that only a few humans and dragons still remained faithful to each other. She quickly chipped in by affirming that she was part of those few because she liked dragons a lot and could never betray them even though she had never met one. Azi was more than relieved and happy when he heard that part. He felt so honored that there was more than one faithful human who he could trust. Carter just smiled at Azi with joy that Azi could now trust Yamina. For Carter, he had already trusted her from when she told of her experiences with Grandpa. It was more than obvious she knew who his Grandpa was. He was cocksure she couldn't have made up that story. Yamina ended her story by saying that there was a legend of a safe place where dragons could live peacefully without fear. The boys didn't realize that was the end of the story because they were eager and anxious to know where the safe place was exactly. They were shocked when they heard Yamina say that was the end of the folklore. It was like taking someone so high then pushing the person down. Carter didn't give up as he decided to question her hoping to get clues of their destination. Azi just shook his head in surprise because he didn't see that question coming from Carter. He was happy and fulfilled that Carter applied a lot of wisdom and that, at last, they were going to know their exact and specific destination.

It was as if they were finally going to win a jackpot. Azi thought to himself that Yamina, whom he felt was up to no good, was actually up to a lot of good. She was actually up to answering his prayers. Her response was going to be that key. To the boy's utmost disappointment, her answers where vague and she let them down. She pulled down their really high hopes. According to Yamina, Grandpa mentioned the safe place once. Grandpa said a lot of landmarks would be passed through before the exact location could be gotten to. That was what she remembered! The boys gave a really distressing look as the information was far from what they needed. It was what they knew already. In fact, that was the first thing they set out in their minds. Seeing the unhappy look on the faces of the boys, Yamina felt bad for them even though she didn't understand why they were so interested in knowing more. For the sole reason of always keeping her guests happy as she had been taught, she decided to think deeply if she could remember any additional information. Eureka! She remembered something! The landmarks were between eight and fifteen kilometers from her town *i.e.*, her home. The boys just shook their heads in more disappointment to the complex answer she gave. They just gave her a reluctant smile to encourage her for her efforts.

To their greatest surprise, that wasn't all she remembered. It was like their reluctant smile indeed encouraged her to remember more. Though she didn't know much more about the exact place, she had an idea of how it could be found. She was indeed trying her best to make her guests happy and comfortable. They were eager to listen to her idea hoping that she wouldn't disappoint them this time around. Going on, she also remembered her mother read a lot about dragons in an old library. She even borrowed some books to continue her study on dragons. That explained the pictures of dragons hung around the walls of the parlor. Azi gave a sigh of relief as his fear of Yamina's mother being a dragon hunter had been removed. She explained further that she was sure the old library contained vital information that could be of help in finding out where the safe place for dragons exactly is. Giving a look of expectation, the duo simultaneously asked where the old library was located. She replied that the old library was located in the Duke's castle which contained ancient tones of history and legend. After this explanation, the boys were indeed relieved that the old library was surely the key to the end of the tunnel for them. Carter warmly smiled to her with joy in his heart that he never made a mistake trusting her from the start. His imaginations were really working for him.

Yamina was also happy that her interrogation session was finally over. Unfortunately for her, her guests still had more questions for her. She wasn't totally annoyed because they weren't pests as she thought they would be since they kept her company. She was already getting bored to death before their arrival. She was beginning to give up on her search before she decided to stroll out with her dad's vehicle. She was just driving around the village to ease her boredom since she really didn't have any close friends when she met the two dramatic boys. Even if the necklace didn't glow or shine that day she would have still helped the boys. Luckily for the duo, her hobby was helping people in distress. Besides they looked interesting and dramatic especially with their facial expression, argumentative gestures, and gesticulations, she was already getting carried away with her thoughts when the persistent call of her name by the boys jerked her back to reality. She apologized and continued her explanation by adding that her mother was a scholar there apart from the fact that she works there. The boys were shocked because her answer was quite different from what they asked her. Their question was about strangers to the town. Yamina just smiled at the degree of her distraction.

She apologized again although she realized that her wrong answer was still useful in giving the correct answer. She continued by adding that due to the information she gave earlier, she had been given the permission to use the library whenever she wanted as her mother's daughter. In addition, she was also permitted to take in two of her friends. It made matters easy for her since they were exactly two on the dot. Carter and Azi were extremely happy with the news they just heard. Yamina was really an immense help to them. To Carter, she had proven worthy to handle their trust. It was like every second that passed by, he felt more at ease with her. He felt he could trust her more and more, over and over. Carter couldn't just thank her enough, so he thanked her all over again. Yamina was just smiling but to her, she felt it was nothing *i.e.*, it wasn't a big deal in anyway. The three had been through with their meal a long time ago. In fact, their conversation started after they all finished their meal. At this juncture, she thought it wise to clear the dishes to the kitchen. She should have done that much more earlier but she had been held down by the un-ending conversation and interrogation. At a point in the question and answer session, Yamina concluded in her mind that the boys' reason for the questions was because of young age curiosity. It was normal for children of that age to be curious about what went on in their environment.

She also felt that in addition, they must have been curious to know the dragons Carter's Grandpa always talked about. Since the zoo or habitat for dragons was the sanctuary land, they were curious to know where it was located. After her imagined conclusion, she felt at ease with herself as she washed the dishes in the kitchen. Carter kept on whispering something into Azi's ears as Yamina came back to the parlor after being done with the dishes. She had something extra awaiting her. She announced that she wanted to lead them to the room they would spent the night when Carter interrupted her by saying that they had something important to tell her. She was scared at first hand and had a wide range of thoughts of what they could possibly want to tell her. Carter took a deep breath and sighed heavily as he started narrating the whole truth to her. He totally revealed Azi's true identity and their mission to find sanctuary land for dragons. He also explained Korvis' part in the whole story and what he did part in through the whole story and what he did to Dara, Azi's father. He additionally made mention of how Dara was a good father to Azi and Dara's closeness with Grandpa before the duos demise. Yamina was shocked beyond measure at all she heard. Azi transformed into his real form. That was the height of it for Yamina. Yamina found it extremely unbelievable to believe. She was in deep shock at what she had just heard and saw. It was like she was seeing a movie with a lot of stunts. Never had Yamina, in her wildest imagination, ever think that dragons ever existed to her; all stories about dragons were nothing but folklore. It was now shocking that dragons not only existed but a live one was standing right in front of her. She didn't know whether to be scared or angry amidst the lies she had earlier been fed with. Carter went on as he apologized with Azi for lying to her at first. They explained their reasons which Korvis was a center of amidst other dragon hunters. She tried to calm herself down as she rushed to the kitchen to drink water to relieve herself. As the mature girl that Yamina was, it didn't take long for her to forgive and understand they so he explained what they were whispering to themselves earlier she in turn appreciated that for their trust and promised that their secret was safe with her. Carter thought to himself that they could now sleep with peace of mind without fear of being caught. It was as if a burden was lifted off his shoulders. Carter was sure within himself that what they had just done was the right thing to do. Alas, every folklore had some truth to it. They weren't all just make–believe stories.

That wasn't all for the night as Carter and Azi thought. There was something more as Yamina also had something extra to say. She was more than honored and over joyed that they could confide in her. Since they were that brave, she decided to exchange such act. She confided in them about her mother. It was at this moment that Carter and Azi realized that when Yamina was telling her original story, she left her mother out. The only thing they could remember was that her mother was a scholar, studied about dragons and worked at the old library. She explained that the story was a simple one. Barely a year after Grandpa left them, something unfortunate happened. On that fateful day, her mother didn't come back from the library like she used to every evening. All night, her mother was missing. Yamina went to the library the next morning and other places to search for her mother all to no avail at the library. She was crushed in spirit because until that very night she was discussing with Carter and Azi her mother was still nowhere to be found. That explained why she was living alone in such a big house. Tears freely fell from her eyes as she ended her story. The boys consoled her to the best of their ability. She was still filled with a lot of hope that she would find her mother someday. She braced herself as they planned to go the library the next day. What a long night….

CHAPTER SIX

They go to the library and discover a scroll.

"Do we really have to be dressed like servants? I thought you said we were going to the library," Carter asked.

"Can we just go without you asking questions, Carter? You ask too many questions and they have really become unbecoming," Yamina said as she motioned to Carter to hold his peace.

"This boy is just too inquisitive, is he always this way?" Azi asked Yamina who instead waved aside the question.

"The two of you had better listen carefully. You have to follow my instructions carefully particularly when we are with the librarian so that we don't get caught," she said facing the boys with an out-stretched middle index finger that was pointed at them.

They headed for the library and luckily, on arrival, the librarian was not at the entrance so they could maneuver and get inside the library without any confrontation.

They sneaked into the library and just when they thought they had escaped being seen by the librarian, a thick voice rustled above them as it filled the air.

"Who are you? And what do you want around here?" the librarian asked.

"Good afternoon sir, I am here on my mother's request to do some research using the books available in this library. We did not meet anyone on the front desk when we arrived and that is why it seems like we are intruding," Yamina answered the librarian as she tried to hide the real reason for their coming to the library.

"Ok then. Please follow me." The librarian beckoned to them as he led them into an inner chamber that was an extension of the building housing the library.

As they got there, Carter and Azi started to ransack the shelves making it appear as if they were really looking for books waiting until the time the librarian leaves for other duties.

"C'mon guys let's hurry over there," Yamina said in a hushed tone pointing to another room in the library as the librarian went on with his business. As they approached the door, they could tell that activities of any sort had not happened around the door. They opened the door and were greeted by cobwebs and a dust filled room.

"Where is this, Yamina?" the ever-curious Carter asked.

"Maybe some room people don't visit," Azi replied almost immediately in a tone that meant shut up.

Yamina soon found the switch and then she turned on the light in the room. The room was filled with old books, scrolls and things that neither Azi nor Carter could recognize. "When and how did you find this place?" Azi asked.

"When my grandfather was alive, he used to bring me here with him whenever he came to tutor his classes. Here are some of the books he used in teaching about dragon lore. Be careful as you bring that out," Yamina said. Her attention had been caught by Carter who was reaching out to pick up a book.

Carter frowned in annoyance.

"I can't read anything here. I don't understand the lettering," he cried out. Yamina grabs the book quickly from Carter as she tries to read the book together with Azi.

"I will not be able to read about dragons? There should be a simpler language," Carter complained out loud to himself. "How can Azi read a book I can't?" Carter asked as he hovered around Yamina. Yamina told him off out rightly – "why don't you play around as we concentrate on this book."

He leaves quietly with his head held down and disappointment written all over him. He starts walking around the room to see if he would find a book written in a simpler language he could comprehend.

Carter walks round the room opening any book that catches his fancy. "Maybe I can find simpler books up there?" he said to himself.

As he looked around, his eyes caught a book in a tight corner. He let out a loud squeal as he hurried up the ladder to look closely at what he had found.

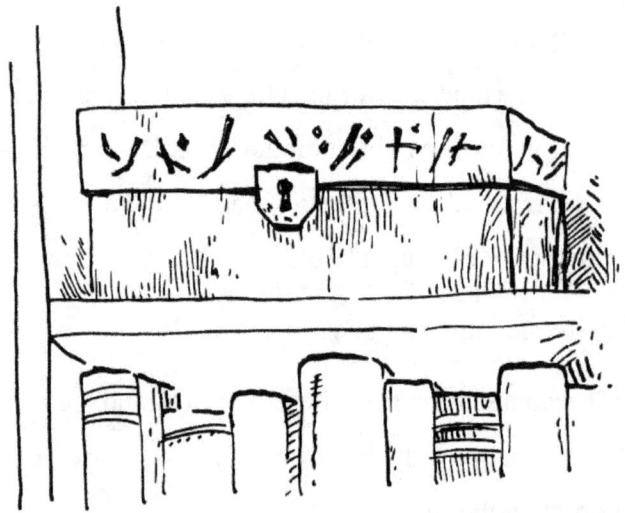

"Where have I seen these symbols? They look so familiar." he said to himself. "My necklace! Yes, my necklace," he shouts out loud. He hurriedly brings the box down from the shelf.

"Take it easy," Yamina said while Azi collected the box from him.

"What happened to your necklace? Is it in the box and how did it get there?" Azi asked.

"No," he answered, as he took off the necklace from his neck. "This box has the same symbols as my necklace and maybe it is the key to opening it," Carter said.

"That is not possible. Grandpa would never give you such a precious key to carry around carelessly," Yamina said leaving Azi and Carter to play around.

Azi collects the necklace and inserts it into the box. "It's not opening, Carter. Yamina was right about the necklace after all."

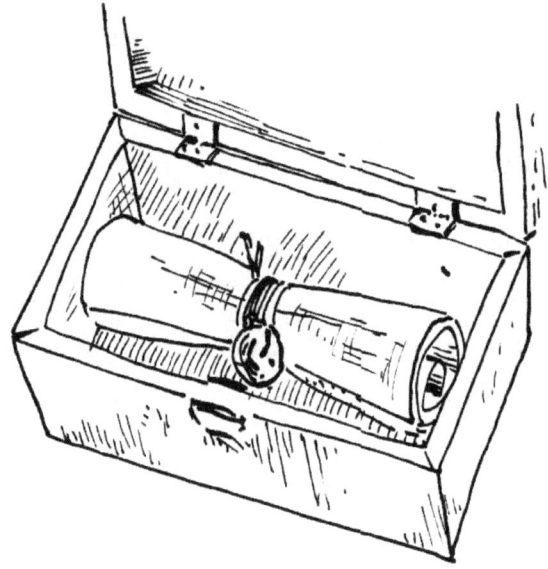

Carter grabbed the keys and tried opening the box which opened immediately.

"I unlocked it!" he shouted with joy and excitement.

"What is inside?" Yamina and Azi asked simultaneously.

"It's a scroll," he replied.

"What is this? It looks so much different from anything I have ever read here. I have read a lot of books here but this does not look familiar to me. I can't read this," Yamina said.

Azi collected the book from her. "This is a dragon's writing," Azi said smiling.

"Dragons write too?" Carter asked looking really shocked.

"Yes, they do, dragons write with their claws and that is why if you look closely you'd see that the lettering is thicker and scratchier than what a pen would do."

Carter and Yamina nodded in agreement with what Azi had said.

"I'll read what the scroll says out to you." Azi said. "There is a land of dragons where no human has ever set foot, the land where dragons lived before they ventured out into the human's world." Azi's face lit up as he read the words again and again.

"Maybe there is another world like where I come from that dragons live in and maybe Azi could get there using magic of dragon stones." Carter said.

"So, that means I am not the only one left. Is there any way to locate where this world is? I need to find them." Azi said to himself.

He quickly looks through the scroll to see if he could find any clues for a direction.

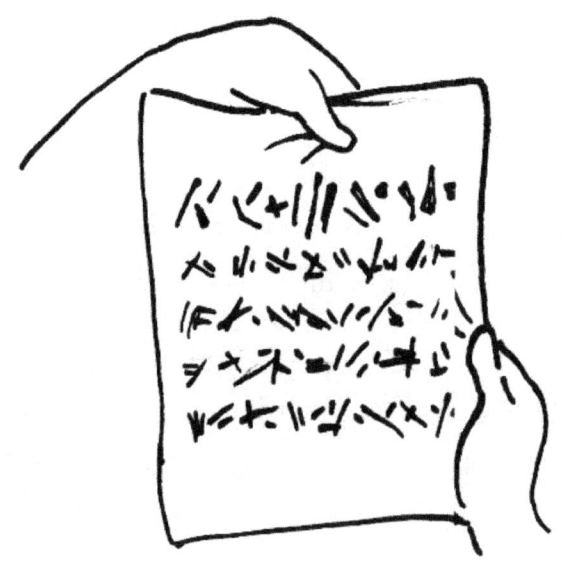

"Yamina, do you understand what these symbols mean?" Azi asked, showing the scroll to Yamina.

"Of course not. I am not a dragon. I don't know these symbols." Yamina replied.

"Ok then, just take down the notes." Azi said to Yamina. She quickly gets some paper to write on as she took down the points.

"Shhh, I can hear footsteps approaching. Carter why don't you look out and see whoever is coming?"

Carter tiptoed to the door and looked around but there was no one there.

"All the same guys, I think its best we hurry up so we don't get caught here," Carter said.

Azi returned the box to where Carter had collected it from and they quickly put everything back in its place. Quietly, they closed the door leading back to the room and went back into the library, making it seem as if they had been reading all day and were ready to leave for home.

They left for Yamina's house with a bigger task ahead of them. They were to decipher the clues they could get from the book in the library. They had to find a way to get Azi back to the other dragons.

CHAPTER SEVEN

Having a map to follow, the trio continue onto the Land of the Dragons.

As they're making their way through the castle courtyard, Azi stiffens. He's spotted their nemesis, Korvis, talking to a man that Yamina tells them in a whisper is the duke. They creep closer and hear Korvis telling the duke about the dragon in the area – probably in the town itself. The duke gives out orders to block all the town gates and shut down the bridge.

The kids' only hope is to make it to the bridge before the duke's guards. They just must get out of the castle grounds without Korvis or his band of dragon hunters spotting them.

The kids are spotted as they're leaving the castle. Korvis, the dragon hunters, the duke's guards, *etc.* all give chase. The kids make it out of the castle but get trapped inside the city. They must come up with a clever plan to get across the river. It works.

They narrowly escape, going back to Yamina's house to get themselves organized, and leave on the next segment of their journey.

APPENDIX
DRAWINGS YOU MAY COLOR

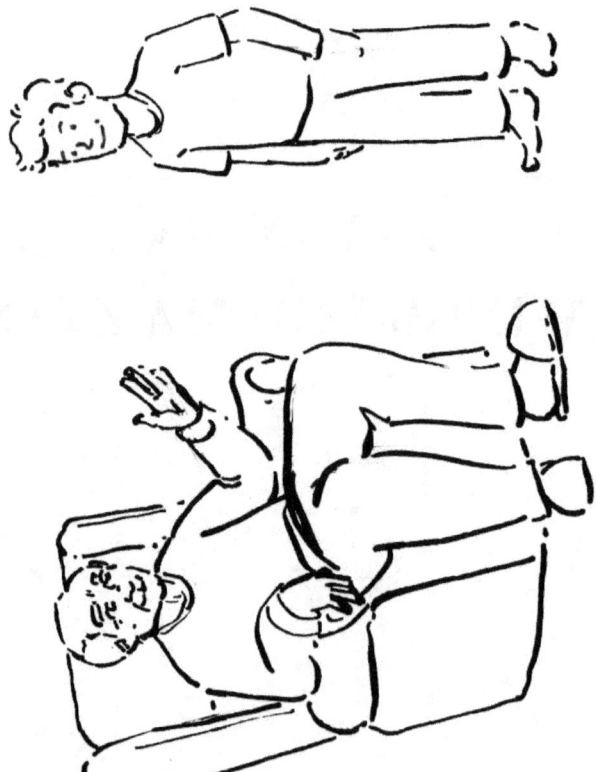

Figure 1: Carter and his Grandpa

Figure 2: Box left to Carter by his Grandpa

Figure 3 Surprised Carter

Figure 4: Young Azi

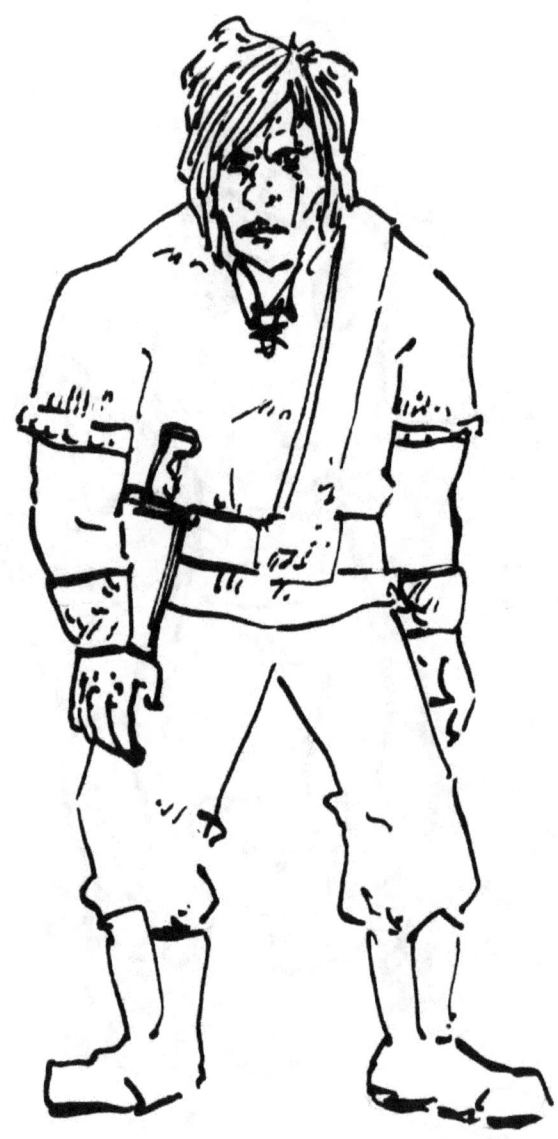

Figure 5: Korvis, Dragon Hunter

Figure 6: Carter with mature Azi

Figure 7: Tara, Azi's mother

Figure 8 A Bushbabby

Figure 9 Carter as a Dragon

Figure 10 Farm Scene

Figure 11 Inn Keeper

Figure 12 Carter and Azi dressed as performers

Figure 13 Naptime

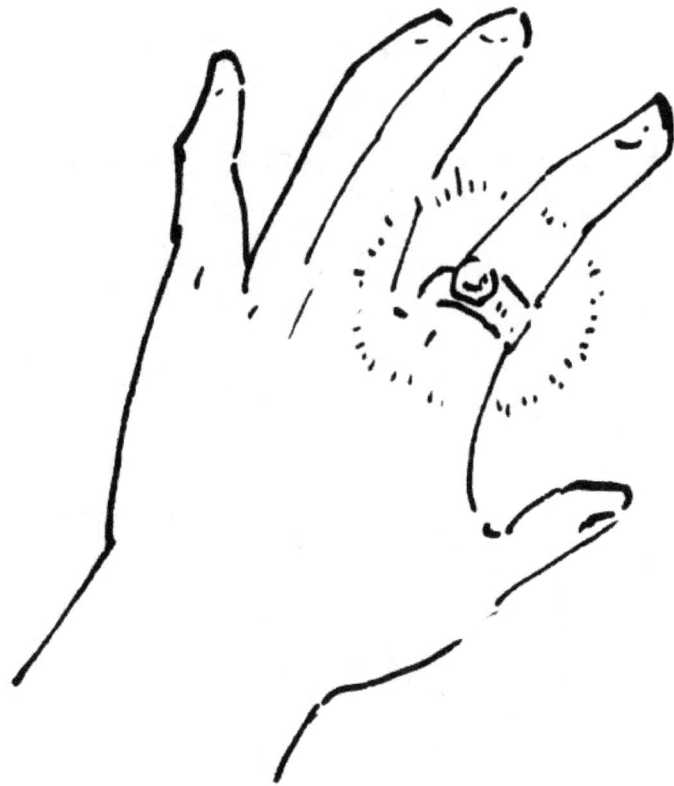

Figure 14 Ring Glowing

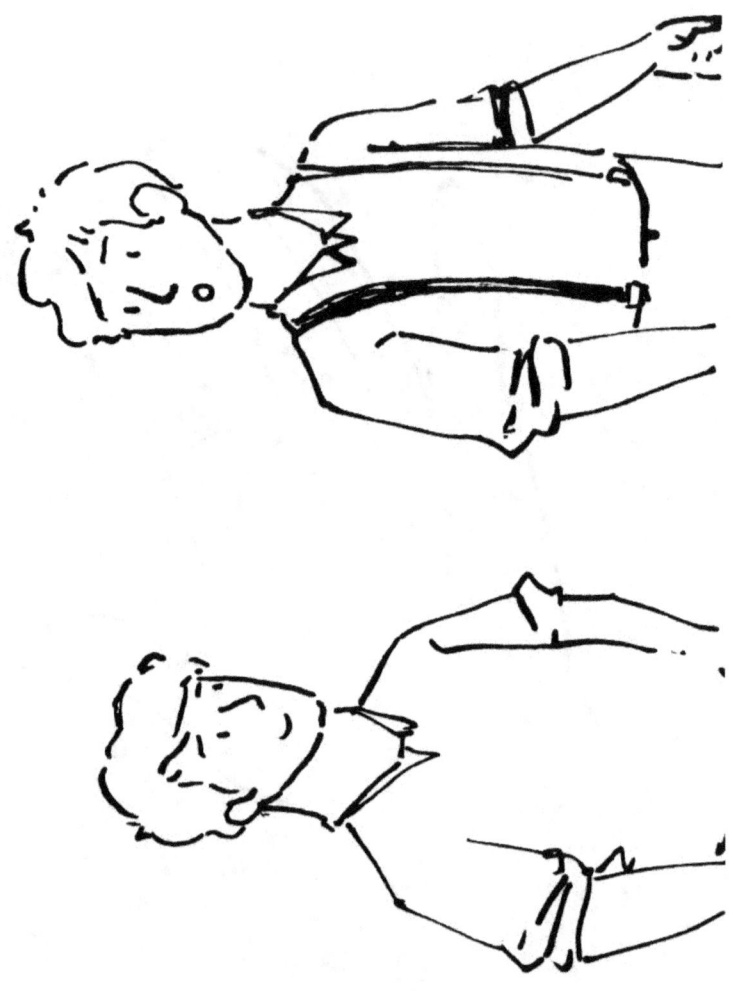

Figure 15 Azi with Carter in the form of a human

Figure 16 Azi breathing fire

Figure 17 Time to eat at the Inn

Figure 18 Korvis rushing for Carter and Azi

Figure 19 Carter is captured

Figure 20 Carter running into Korvis

Figure 21 Azi attacking Korvis

Figure 22 Nap time on some pond fronds

Figure 23 Azi laughing

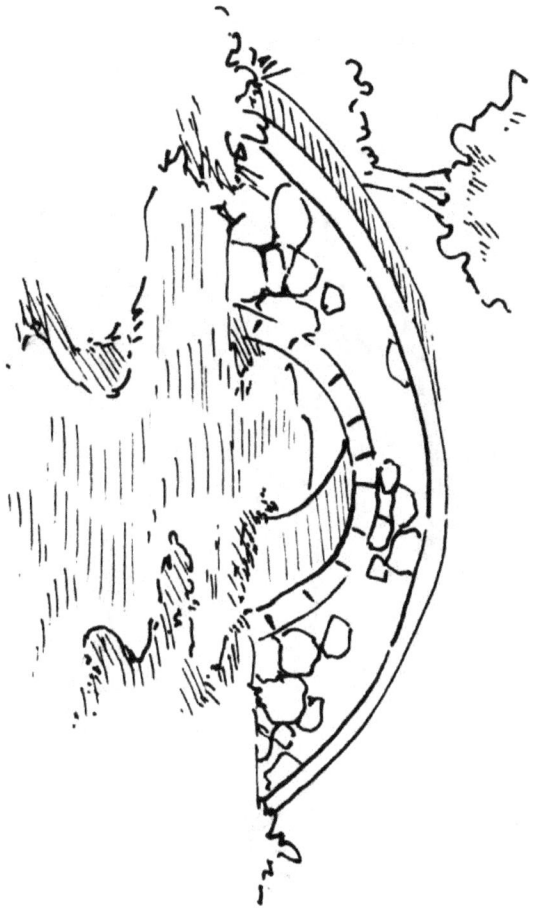

Figure 24 Picturesque Bridge

Figure 25 Carter and Azi talking

Figure 26 Korvis sights Carter and Azi

Figure 27 Korvis gives chase after Carter and Azi

Figure 28 Women of the village at the well

Figure 29 A Car Stops to Pick Them Up

Figure 30 The female driver surprises Azi

Figure 31 Yamina's Home

Figure 32 Relaxing in the Parlor

Figure 33 Yamina

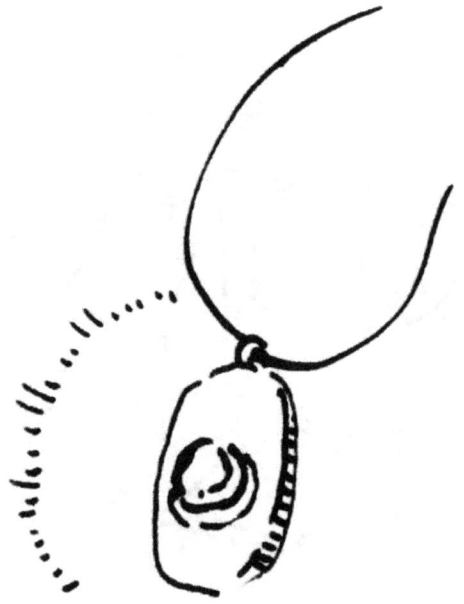

Figure 34 Yamina's Necklace

Figure 35 Grandpa tutoring Yamina

Figure 36 Carter and Azi crying while listening to Yamina's story

Figure 37 Dragons and humans once lived in perfect harmony

Figure 38 Carter and Azi happy

Figure 39 Yamina doing the dishes

Figure 40 Yamina telling Carter and Azi about the library

Figure 41 Yamina at the library with Carter and Azi disguised as servants

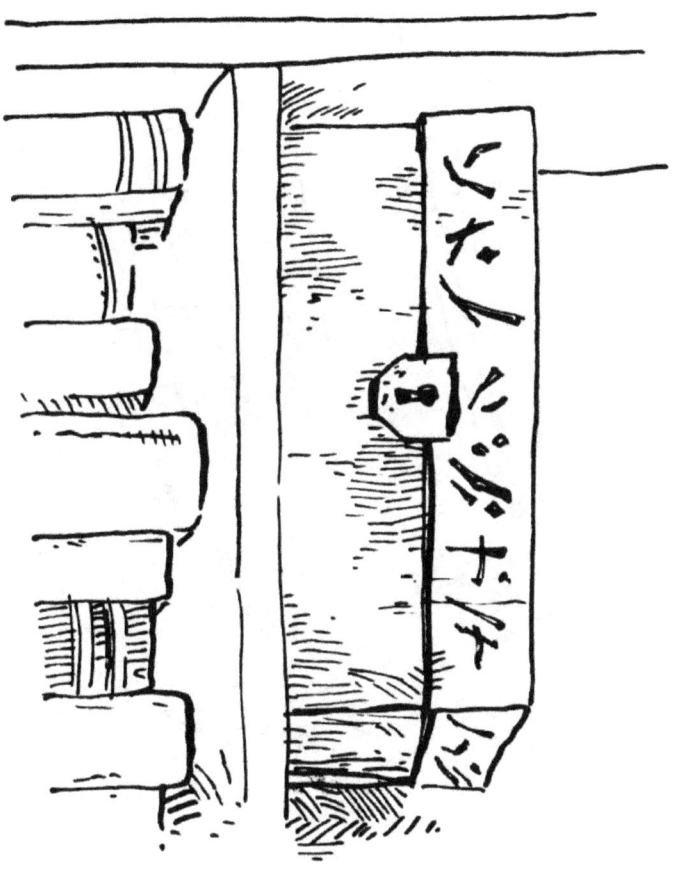

Figure 42 Mysterious box found on a shelf

Figure 43 They find a scroll in the box

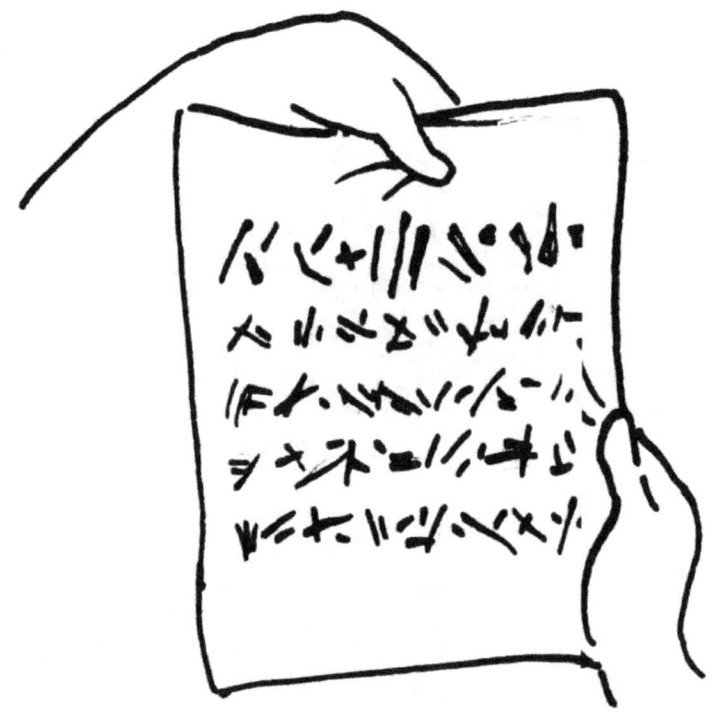

Figure 44 The mysterious scroll with dragon writings on it.

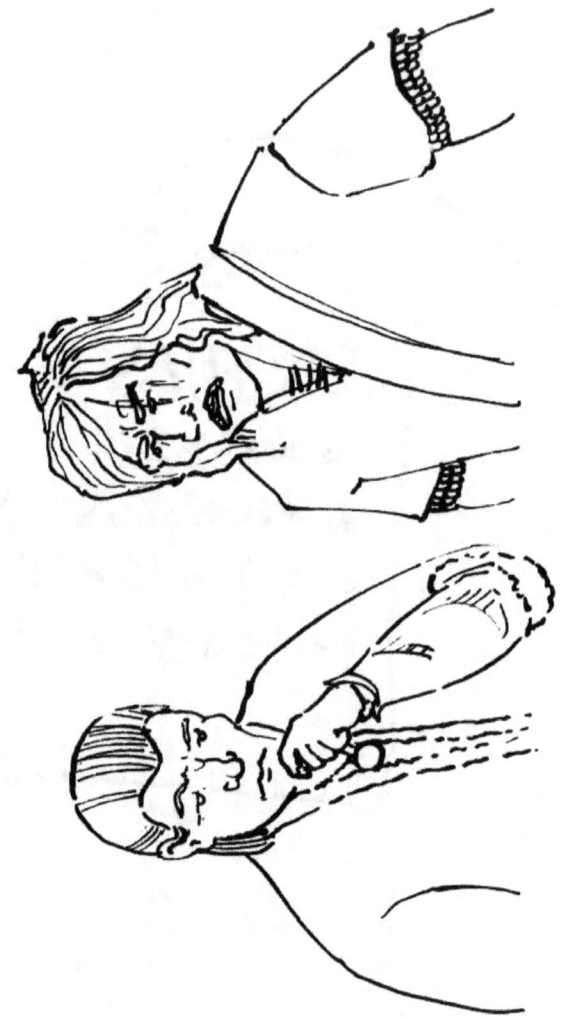

Figure 45 The Duke and Korvis talking.

Figure 46 The Chase is on.